THE
VOYAGE
OF
PATIENCE
GOODSPEED

HEATHER VOGEL FREDERICK

Simon & Schuster Books for Young Readers
New York London Toronto Sydney Singapore

SIMON & SCHUSTER BOOKS FOR YOUNG READERS
An imprint of Simon & Schuster Children's Publishing Division
1230 Avenue of the Americas, New York, NY 10020

Book design by Russell Gordon
The text for this book is set in Minister.
Printed in the United States of America

2 4 6 8 10 9 7 5 3 1

Library of Congress Cataloging-in-Publication Data
Frederick, Heather Vogel.
The voyage of Patience Goodspeed / by Heather Vogel Frederick.
p. cm.
Summary: Following their mother's death in Nantucket, Captain Goodspeed brings twelve-year-old Patience and six-year-old Tad aboard his whaling ship, where a new crew member incites a mutiny and Patience puts her mathematical ability to good use.
ISBN 0-689-84851-X
[1. Seafaring life—Fiction. 2. Whaling—Fiction. 3. Mutiny—Fiction. 4. Fathers and daughters—Fiction. 5. Fathers and sons—Fiction. 6. Navigation—Fiction.] I. Title.
PZ7.F87217 Vo 2002
[Fic]—dc21
2001049039

FIRST
EDITION

EDITOR'S NOTE: Please refer to the author's note, Patience's delicious recipes, and a glossary of nautical terms on pages 214-222.

For my mother

One

If ever I return again
A solemn vow I'll take
That I'll never go a-whaling,
My liberty to stake.
I will stay at home
And I will roam no more,
For the pleasures are but few my boys,
Far from our native shore.

—*The Whaleman's Lament*

"Absolutely, positively not!" roared my father in a voice meant to be heard through the teeth of a Cape Horn gale.

I glanced across the breakfast table at my little brother. His face was puckered, and I could tell he was on the brink of tears. Papa had been ashore less than a month, and Thaddeus, who was only just six, was still unaccustomed to his blustering.

"But Papa," I said meekly, "it was Mama's particular wish that I should study with Miss Mitchell."

My father reached over and harpooned a sausage from the serving platter.

"Thunder and lightning, Patience!" he cried, shaking his fork at me for emphasis. "I've said no and I mean no. You and Thaddeus will accompany me aboard the *Morning Star* when she sails again."

Martha Russell, our housekeeper, appeared in the doorway bearing a basket of blueberry muffins.

"A whaling ship is no place for children," she muttered under her breath, scowling, as she trundled toward us. As round as a whale oil barrel and wreathed with gray curls, Martha had been with us since I was born and considered herself one of the family.

Papa fixed her with a steely gaze.

"I don't recall asking for your opinion, Martha," he said severely.

She merely sniffed and, poking a finger into my brother's side to make him sit up straight in his chair, quit the room again.

I slipped a piece of sausage under the table to my cat, Patches. The three of us had been going back and forth on this tack for days. Obviously it was time to try another.

Before I could do so, however, Papa continued in a milder tone, "I received a letter from your Aunt Anne yesterday. At my request she is coming to Nantucket to join us for a few weeks. She'll be arriving on the packet from Boston this Friday."

Thaddeus and I exchanged a glance. Aunt Anne! Though we had never met Papa's elder sister, we had heard much about her. Headmistress of Miss Good-speed's School for Young Ladies, she was a frightful bluestocking, according to Papa—though Mama had quite admired her independent sister-in-law's scholarly ways.

I suspected that Aunt Anne's visit was more than just a social call. From the smug expression on his face, Papa clearly had something up his sleeve.

I hoped he wasn't going to announce that he was planning to marry again. There was certainly no shortage of widows on our island. Martha was correct in her assertion that whaling was a dangerous business, and many a ship that sailed from our little harbor was never heard from again, or returned bearing news of some tragedy, from fearsome storms off Cape Horn and stove whaleboats to deadly tropical fevers. No, widows we had aplenty, and since Papa's return I had watched more than a few preen in his presence. He was not yet forty, his black hair and beard only lightly salted with gray, and although the light in his eyes, as blue as the sea off 'Sconset in June, had dimmed since my mother's death, still, he was a well-looking man.

"Marketable," Martha had described him to old Mrs. Starbuck next door, as if Papa were a turnip bound for the greengrocers.

I did not think I would like a new mother. My

heart still ached so with missing Mama that there were times I feared it would burst from my chest and fly away. No, my wounds were still too raw, and so, I believed, were Papa's. Grief had settled over him like one of the creeping gray fogs for which our island is so famous.

Papa was away when Mama died, still three months from home on the last leg of his return voyage. The captain of a whaling ship, he had to leave us for years at a time to hunt the great leviathans whose prized oil fired lamps and lighthouses the world around and furnished our livelihood. The profits from his whaling cruises built our tidy, gray-shingled house, planted our apple tree, purchased our cow, our chickens, the seeds for our vegetable garden—in fact, everything in our happy home, or a home that was happy until Mama died, and Papa returned, a somber stranger given to outbursts of temper.

I understood why Martha and others in our circle of acquaintances were eager to see Papa married again. Grief made people uncomfortable. They didn't know how to behave in its presence, and expected it to be a temporary affliction, like a head cold or the chicken pox, especially if you were a child.

I heard the things they said about Thaddeus and me when they thought I wasn't listening. "Poor little motherless things" no sooner out of their mouths than they would nod sagely and add, "but they're young, and will soon get over it." How could they see inside my heart and know how I felt?

And how could they see inside Papa? Like me, he kept his face shuttered, and his grief only leaked out in the silences.

Meanwhile, he seemed oblivious to the admiring glances cast his way by Nantucket's eligible young widows. He accepted their pies, their chowders, their homemade jams and jellies with an absentminded politeness they must have found infuriating. How he, a fisherman by trade, managed not to notice the bait that was continually dangled before him was truly remarkable. Why, just yesterday I had happened to glance from my bedroom window to see Fanny Starbuck, Mrs. Starbuck's pretty but deeply stupid daughter-in-law, widowed last year when her husband was swept overboard in a gale, standing on our doorstep bold as brass. In one hand she held a loaf of freshly baked bread while with the other she fiddled with her dress, patting and plumping and arranging herself like a flounder on a platter. My father answered her knock, took the bread, thanked her courteously, and then shut the door in her face. I had to bite my tongue to keep from laughing out loud.

No, marriage was not on his mind, of that I was sure. What scheme, then, could he be hatching, and why had he summoned Aunt Anne from Boston?

Papa didn't leave us in suspense.

"When the *Morning Star* sails again my sister will accompany us," he announced. "She will give up her duties at the academy"—he wrinkled his nose slightly at the mention of her school—"in order to care for Thaddeus. And you, Patience, will be a comfort and a solace to her."

"But I do not wish to be a comfort and a solace!" I cried, springing to my feet in protest. Particularly not to my Aunt Anne, I wanted to add, but held my tongue. From all accounts, she was just like my father, prickly and proud. The thought of being imprisoned aboard a ship with the two of them was appalling. "I want to stay here, on Nantucket, as Mama and I planned, and attend Miss Mitchell's school!"

Papa held up his hand in warning. "I am the captain of this ship—I mean the head of this family—and my mind is made up," he said firmly. "We stay together, and you and Thaddeus will sail with me."

Stunned by his slip of the tongue—was I just one of his crew to be ordered about?—I was unable to hold back the hot words that streamed out of me now like a floodtide.

"Why didn't we stay together before, then?" I said bitterly. "Perhaps if we had, and if you hadn't gone sailing off again, Mama wouldn't have taken ill and would still be here with us!"

Papa's face creased with pain, and I could have bitten my tongue off at my hasty words. His distress turned quickly to anger, however.

"That's enough, Patience!" he thundered.

"But it's not fair, Papa! I don't wish to go to sea. Why can't you just take Thaddeus and leave me here with Martha?"

Why couldn't Papa consult my desires and wishes, and not just his own? Why couldn't he see that it wasn't just my schooling, but that I needed to be here, in this house, with all its reminders of Mama's gentle spirit? If I went to sea, I feared I would lose her all over again, and my heart's invisible wounds would never heal.

But such things are not easily said, and Papa was adamant. I would not be allowed to remain behind on any account. And I was banished to my room for the remainder of the morning for my impertinence.

Two

A life on the ocean wave,
A home on the rolling deep,
Where the scattered waters roar
And the winds their revels keep.

—*A Life on the Ocean Wave*

Aunt Anne, as it turned out, surprised us all.

"Absolutely, positively not!" she snapped.

From where Thaddeus and I stood in the parlor doorway, freshly scrubbed by Martha and turned out in our Sabbath finery, as was only proper for greeting our father's formidable elder sister, we had a clear view of Papa's face. Seated on the sofa, he stared at his sister, openmouthed as a cod. Obviously this was not the response he had been expecting.

"I know this is a distressing time for you, Isaiah," Aunt Anne continued. "And there's nothing I wouldn't do to help. But I have duties and obligations in Boston, and had you bothered to consult me regarding your intentions, you could have saved yourself the fare of my crossing."

Papa's eyebrows lowered—a sure storm warning—and he began to sputter, but Aunt Anne ignored him. "It's not that I'm not tempted by your offer, brother—

just think of the adventures!—but my place is at my school."

Papa could contain himself no longer. "Thunder and lightning, Anne!" he bellowed, leaping to his feet. "What poppycock are you talking? This isn't a question of adventure, it's a question of family responsibilities. A whaling ship is a dangerous place, and the children need someone to look after them!"

Martha, who was standing in the hall just outside the doorway eavesdropping shamelessly, nodded smugly at this.

"Nonsense," Aunt Anne retorted, clearly not the least bit cowed by Papa's blustering. She turned around in her chair and leveled an appraising glance at Thaddeus and me. "I should think these two could look after themselves very well. Come here, my dears."

Aunt Anne stood up as Thaddeus and I approached. She was indeed formidable, almost as tall as Papa, with the same determined set of black eyebrows and piercing blue eyes. Holding us by our chins, she tilted our heads back slightly, the better to inspect us.

"You are your mother all over again, dear heart," she said to me in a soft undertone.

Her words surprised me. Though it was true that I had inherited Mama's chestnut brown hair, my eyes were blue like Papa's, and on the rare occasion that anyone ever remarked about a resemblance, it was invariably my eyes they noted.

Turning back to my father, Aunt Anne announced in a firm voice, "Patience is nearly thirteen and clearly a capable girl, Isaiah, and Thaddeus looks a sensible lad. They're Goodspeeds through and through, and I can't fathom why you think you need me along to play nursemaid."

Papa began to sputter again, but before he could erupt with further protests, Martha called us to the dinner table. Afterward, at Aunt Anne's request, Thaddeus and I gave her a tour of the island.

Aunt Anne had only been to Nantucket once before, years ago when Papa and Mama were married. Papa was an off-islander, born and bred in Boston like his sister, but he had left the mainland behind when a ship on which he was employed chanced to put ashore here for repairs and he met Mama.

"I fell in love with Nantucket two minutes after I fell in love with your mother," he always used to tell us, back when he still talked about Mama. Since his return, he rarely mentioned her name.

Though it was late September, summer still lingered in the air, and the afternoon sun was warm on our shoulders.

"I always meant to visit Nantucket again," said Aunt Anne, opening her parasol. "But Mother and Father needed me, and then after they were gone, there were my duties at the academy."

My heart lifted at the mention of her school. My aunt was not nearly as starchy as I had imagined, and surely with her high regard for education, once I explained my plight she would come to my aid and convince Papa to leave me ashore.

Aunt Anne displayed a lively curiosity about everything we showed her, particularly our atheneum, where we spent an interminable hour, Thaddeus squirming in his chair, while she and the librarian—Maria Mitchell, my math tutor—engaged in a spirited discussion of the upcoming presidential election.

When we emerged back into the sunlight, Aunt Anne looked thoughtfully at Thaddeus. "I believe you children are in need of some refreshment," she announced.

Thaddeus perked up at this. "Oh yes, please," he said.

I smiled. Even my obstinate little brother was warming to Aunt Anne.

"Would you happen to know of a suitable destination?" she asked.

Nodding happily, Thaddeus took her by the hand

and tugged her in the direction of the harbor. Whenever he went missing, I always knew I could find him there, for the harbor was the heart of our small community, and it was the rare soul who did not take pleasure in watching the great whaling ships as they arrived and departed, or the lighters that ferried their crews and cargos to and from the docks.

The wharves bustled with activity, from the blacksmith's shop, where passersby could observe as men beat glowing metal into harpoons and cutting spades and all the other tools of Papa's trade, to the sailmaker's loft, where stout canvas was fashioned into white wings for whaling vessels. Thaddeus's favorite haunt of all was the chandler's gloomy shop, crowded with try-pots and twine, compasses, spyglasses, lanterns, and all the other paraphernalia needed to outfit a whaling voyage.

Like most boys on Nantucket, my little brother dreamed of going to sea and hunting whales, and Papa's decision couldn't have made him happier. I wished fervently that Papa would notice and take more of an interest in him, but since his return his days were spent shut up in his study, supposedly toiling over important papers, but more often than not simply staring out the window.

It was to the chandler's shop that we were headed, and while Thaddeus secured us some toffee from within—his definition of "refreshment," though perhaps not exactly Aunt Anne's—I broached the subject of my schooling.

"Well, I suppose your father might be persuaded to allow you to accompany me back to Boston," Aunt Anne said doubtfully, after hearing me out. Seeing my chagrined expression at this, she arched a dark eyebrow and added with a wry smile, "but I suspect that's not what you had in mind."

I stared at my toes, embarrassed.

"Your mother wrote me often, you know," Aunt Anne continued. I looked up in surprise. "Yes, Caroline told me all about your mathematical abilities. She expected great things from you, my dear, and she was quite right to engage Miss Mitchell as your tutor. A better one could not be had, not even at Harvard College itself." She paused for a moment, then continued gently, "Still, your father has good reason for wanting you to sail with him. Family ties are a fragile thing, Patience, easily broken. Your mother's death has affected my brother greatly, this anyone can see, and you and Thaddeus will be a great comfort and solace to him."

Her response was discouraging. Why did it seem that everyone wanted *me* to be a comfort and a solace? What about *my* comfort?

Before I could press my case, however, Thaddeus

emerged bearing not only toffee but also a small spy-glass, a present from the shopkeeper.

"Mr. Tilton said I would need it now that I'm going to be a whaleman like Papa," he announced happily, putting it up to his eye and scanning the harbor. "Look! There's Papa's ship!"

"Give us a turn, Tad," I said.

Reluctantly, Thaddeus handed over his new treasure. Sure enough, there was the *Morning Star,* lying quietly at anchor in the deeper waters beyond the treacherous sandbar that spanned the harbor's entrance.

We watched the ships for a while, then turned for home as the sun slanted low on the horizon. Ahead of us, the clink of glass and cutlery mingled with raucous shouts of laughter and drifted through the open door of the Spouter Tavern. As we passed it, Thaddeus (who was still peering through his spyglass not paying the least bit of attention) suddenly collided with a pair of emerging sailors.

"'Ere now, mind where you're going, young jackanapes," said the larger of the two, grabbing my brother by the scruff of his neck and shaking him like a puppy. He was none too steady on his feet, and smelled as if he'd been pickled in a vat of rum.

Thaddeus squirmed in his grasp, flailing his arms and legs.

"Ow!" cried his assailant, as one of my brother's

feet connected with his shin. He shook Thaddeus again, harder this time.

"Toss 'im overboard and teach 'im a lesson," suggested his companion, jerking his thumb toward the edge of the wharf with a snigger.

Aunt Anne stepped forward, closing up her parasol. "You'll do nothing of the sort," she snapped, rapping Thaddeus's captor on the knuckles with its whalebone handle. "Release him at once."

The big fellow dropped Thaddeus like a hot coal. Nursing his wounded hand, he snarled something under his breath and lurched toward Aunt Anne. She held her ground, scowling fiercely. Wielding her parasol once again, she poked him sharply in the ribs. "Clear off now, the two of you, before I report you to the watchman as a public nuisance."

"Come on then, Binyon," said the smaller of the two, grabbing his companion by the arm. "Best not tangle with the law."

"You haven't seen the last of me, you clumsy pup," the other man growled, reluctantly allowing himself to be towed off.

Thaddeus, who had retreated behind me, poked his head out and watched as the men reeled away.

"Thunder and lightning, Aunt Anne!" he said admiringly. "You sounded just like Papa."

"I did, didn't I?" she replied with satisfaction.

"A Goodspeed through and through!" I added, and, buoyed by our triumph, the three of us linked arms and headed happily for home.

The remainder of Aunt Anne's visit sped by far too quickly. As it turned out, Papa was no match for his bossy elder sister, and despite his protests and blustering she continued to refuse to accompany us aboard the *Morning Star*. As the day of her departure drew near, it was finally settled. Aunt Anne would return to Boston, and Thaddeus and I would be going to sea.

Three

A chest that is neither too large nor too small
Is the first thing to which your attention I'll call;
The things to put in it are next to be named
And if I omit some I'm not to be blamed.

—A Fitting Out

"Your father is like to have lost his mind," said Martha irritably. She was in a dither, flying about the house like a large, gray-haired pigeon as she tried to organize us for our imminent voyage. "Why he doesn't see fit to leave the two of you anchored here on Nantucket is beyond me. The idea of it! Taking children on a whaling cruise. He must be mad."

She had been like this for days now, fussing and complaining as she went about her work, with many sighs and tut-tuts and surreptitious swipes at her eyes with the edge of her apron when she thought we weren't looking. Obviously she would much rather have seen Papa married off to silly Fanny Starbuck and Thaddeus and I safe and sound at home, rather than heading to the ends of the earth on a whaling ship. It was all very tiresome, and I found myself looking eagerly for excuses to escape out of the house.

I was stiffly polite to Papa, who stubbornly ignored my continued resistance to his plan. I was altogether miserable as the preparations went forward and sea chests were obtained and filled to bursting with everything Thaddeus and I would need for what would likely be a three-year voyage.

Clothing, of course, suitable for both winter and summer, for we would be sailing from Nantucket around the frigid reaches of Cape Horn and into the balmy tropics. Extra fabric was procured, in Martha's vain hope that I might change my wayward habits with a needle and actually produce something wearable, or at least prove myself capable of patching worn-out garments. Despite Mama's diligent tutelage, I was a woeful seamstress, wrestling so fruitlessly over the years with a series of pitifully ill-favored samplers that she had finally thrown up her hands in defeat. Martha, however, had never given up trying to encourage me in this endeavor.

Books we packed too—the Bible and Mr. Shakespeare naturally, as well as mathematical texts from Miss Mitchell, who was as sorely disappointed as I that I would not be enrolling in her school, novels by James Fenimore Cooper and Mama's favorite, Sir Walter Scott. Toys as well, though few, as Papa warned us there would be little space for fripperies. Thaddeus chose his tin soldiers, and despite broad hints from Martha that I had surely outgrown her, I packed Miranda, the old stuffed doll that Mama made for me when I was Thaddeus's age, missing half her yarn hair and worn out from love. Now that Mama was gone, I had only Miranda with whom to share my secrets, and I could no more leave her behind than I could my memories of Mama.

Papa refused to allow me to bring Patches, however.

"She's an old puss, and unaccustomed to life at sea," he explained. "It would be unkind to try and make her over into a ship's cat."

"She's as settled in her ways as I am in mine," added Martha, patting her gray curls. "We're just two old tabbies destined to sit here by the fire and keep each other company until your return."

Finally, the day came when we were packed and ready. We made the rounds of friends and neighbors to say our farewells, Papa accepting their wishes of "greasy luck"—our Nantucket way of bidding whalemen a profitable voyage, with many barrels of oil—with all the dignity of a departing monarch. Which in a sense he was, as were all whaling captains on the tiny kingdom that was our island.

He even managed to avoid Fanny Starbuck until the day before our departure, I was happy to note, merely lifting his hat to her politely when we finally crossed paths in town. Pretty, yes, but if there was a single original thought rattling around in that empty head of hers it was surely bored from lack of company. With any luck, she would marry some unsuspecting fellow while we were gone and I would be spared her foolish chatter forever.

On the evening prior to our departure, Papa took his leave in order to make the final arrangements aboard the *Morning Star*. After he left, I tossed and turned all night, my thoughts a jumble. Oh, why didn't I have the courage to defy Papa! But what was the use? Even if I were to run away and hide, Papa would find me. And besides, my little brother needed me. It was me he had looked to since Mama's death, not Papa, who was still a stranger to him. I couldn't desert Tad now.

Martha awoke us at dawn, and we tumbled groggily out of bed.

"Come along now, Tad," she said, wrestling my sleepy and protesting brother into the small ell off the kitchen. "Won't do for the captain's son to step aboard looking like an orphan." He emerged a few minutes later, unnaturally clean.

I had bathed the night before, but Martha inspected me closely all the same before reluctantly pronouncing me fit to travel.

She had a poor estimation of shipboard fare and,

convinced we wouldn't see a square meal until we were safely back on Nantucket soil again, had prepared us a breakfast that was clearly meant to tide us over until that day came. The table was piled high with platters of eggs and bacon (some of which made its way to Patches, of course), as well as toast and bannock and even doughnuts, a treat we rarely saw other than at Christmas and birthdays.

Finally, groaning and unable to swallow another crumb, we pushed back from the table and waddled out to the doorstep where the dray that would ferry us down to the wharf awaited.

"Good-bye, Patches," I said, bending down to give my cat one last pat. "Take good care of Martha."

As I stood up again, the tears I had been holding back all morning finally spilled over.

"You poor mites!" Martha cried, pressing us to her ample bosom. "I hope your father knows what he's doing!"

Thaddeus and I embraced her warmly in return. Martha was a trial sometimes, and far too broody since Mama died, but if the truth were told, we would miss her dreadfully. With one last kiss she surrendered us to the driver, and we climbed up onto the wooden seat beside him.

"Mind you don't forget to wear your flannel undergarments round the Horn!" she called loudly, much to my chagrin. The driver suppressed a smirk. "And write to us often!"

She waved her handkerchief in farewell, calling out more last-minute words of advice as we clip-clopped down the lane toward town.

I turned in my seat, gazing back for one last time at the only home I had ever known, the home that sang "Mama" to me in every nook and cranny, the home that was my safe harbor. I felt as if my heart would break.

We passed the town crier, who called out "A fine day and a fair wind! The *Morning Star* sails with the afternoon tide!" and Thaddeus poked me in the ribs.

"Look, there she is!" he said.

Pride filled me in spite of myself as I caught sight of the vessel that was to be our home for the next three years. The *Morning Star* was a handsome, three-masted bark, freshly painted a deep bottle green, with sails as white as Mama's bedsheets on washing day furled neatly on the yards. The stars and stripes fluttered at the peak of one of her masts.

Despite the early hour, the streets were crowded with wagons and carts that rumbled and clattered noisily over the cobblestones, and our driver made his way carefully through the throngs of men who called loudly to one another as they loaded and unloaded the schooners and sloops tied up along the dock.

Squeezed in beside me, Thaddeus fairly vibrated with excitement, fingers drumming on the wooden plank that served as a seat. I glanced at him sharply, hoping that my stern lectures about proper behavior had made an impression.

"Whoa there!" said the driver, reining in his mule alongside the sleek lighter that was to take us out to where the *Morning Star* was anchored. He climbed down from his seat, then lifted Thaddeus and me by turn to the ground.

"There you go, miss," he said, depositing our trunks beside me. I thanked him and looked about for Papa.

Keyed into a high state of agitation, Thaddeus was unable to contain himself any longer, and slipping his hand from my grasp scampered nimbly up the gangplank.

"Thaddeus Goodspeed! You come back here this minute!" I called furiously.

Jeremiah Folger, Mama's first cousin and Papa's first mate, appeared at the rail and neatly intercepted my brother, grabbing him firmly by the collar.

"Good morning, Cousin Patience!" he shouted down to me. "Leave your things for the hands and step aboard."

Glancing gingerly down at the dark water that lapped against the pilings of the dock, I stepped onto the narrow gangplank and made my way to the *Desdemona*'s deck.

"Good morning, Cousin Jeremiah," I said, a little breathlessly.

"A happy day, that finds you and your brother joining us," he replied, clasping me warmly by the hand. "Children bring good luck to whaling ships, you know."

Mama always said that Cousin Jeremiah could charm the fuzz off a peach. His quick smile and cheerful nature put everyone at ease—even Papa, with whom he had sailed now on a number of voyages. A town wag had dubbed them "the two prophets"—on account of their Christian names, I supposed, rather than any gift of divination.

The three of us stood at the rail and watched as the dockworkers loaded the last of the supplies bound for the *Morning Star*—casks of rice and Indian meal, coffee and tea, a barrel of nails, and wood to fire the galley stove and tryworks. At last they were finished, and the lines that tethered us to the dock cast off for our short sail to the outer harbor.

Papa was nowhere in sight as Thaddeus and I, hauled up like two sacks of flour, were transferred aboard the *Morning Star*, but Cousin Jeremiah steered us aft toward the deckhouse where we found him seated at a table, a sheaf of papers in one hand and a pen in the other.

"These two lubbers want to sign on for a whaling cruise," said Cousin Jeremiah solemnly.

"Do they now?" Papa replied, glancing up at us. He ignored the mutinous expression on my face. "Well, let's take a look at them."

He pretended to inspect us, twirling us around and prodding Thaddeus's arms for muscles.

"A mite scrawny, but nothing that a few weeks of salt horse and hardtack won't cure," said Papa with a wink. The prospect of returning to sea had clearly buoyed his spirits. "They'll do. You may show them to their quarters, Mr. Folger."

"Aye, sir!" Cousin Jeremiah hustled us further aft as Papa added, "I'll come below and see how you're settling in when I'm finished here."

We were led down the companionway stairs to a small room illuminated by a glass skylight above.

"This is the main cabin," explained Cousin Jeremiah, "and this is where we take our meals."

He pointed to a table in the center of the room. It was surrounded by benches, and through its center, like a tree, sprouted the base of a mast.

"That's the mizzenmast," said Cousin Jeremiah, anticipating my question. "The *Morning Star* has two others besides—the mainmast amidships, and the foremast near the bow."

While I digested this information, he opened a door in the wall behind him. "And this is your father's day cabin," he said.

The space was surprisingly small. The words "day cabin" sounded grand, but I found I could walk from one end to the other in just eight paces. A narrow desk hugged the interior wall, flanked by bookshelves equipped with wooden bars—to keep the contents from spilling out in rough seas, Cousin Jeremiah explained. Facing the desk was a broad, mullioned window set above a red velvet sofa.

Thaddeus clambered up and opened it. A fresh breeze wafted in, and he leaned out curiously.

"Thaddeus!" I said crossly, grabbing him by the arm and hauling him back to safety. "Have you forgotten what I told you already?"

Cousin Jeremiah opened an adjoining door to the right—I would have to learn to say "starboard"—and we followed him into what would be our sleeping quarters for the next three years.

Our stateroom was remarkably tiny, but snugly fitted, with drawers and shelves neatly wedged into every possible inch of space. A china basin rested in a niche atop a small dresser; inside was a pitcher for washing. Stacked against the inside wall were a pair of bunks shielded by latticework—clearly meant for Thaddeus and me—while a longer, single bunk was braced against the outside wall for Papa. Above it hung a compass.

"What's that for?" asked Thaddeus.

"So your Papa can tell which direction we're sailing in at any time of day or night," Cousin Jeremiah replied.

Wide-eyed with delight, Thaddeus raced about opening doors and peeking into drawers.

"Patience! Come and see!" he crowed.

I crossed to where he stood by a large cupboard. Inside, steps led up to a hole cut in a plank, through which the wind whistled. Leaning over, I could see water far below. It was obviously our privy. I wrinkled my nose, and Cousin Jeremiah laughed.

"I'll leave you to unpack," he said, as a sailor appeared with our belongings.

"Can I have the top bunk, Patience?" asked Thaddeus.

"May I," I corrected him absently, as I bent to open my sea chest. "Yes, you may."

Thaddeus climbed up and flung himself down on his new bunk with a sigh of contentment. The windowless cabin was awash in a faint glow from light that filtered through a sort of prism that jutted down from the ceiling above like a glass icicle. It was a bit eerie, and I wondered if I would grow accustomed to it.

Overhead, the pounding of feet on the deck, the loud voices of the crew, and the clash of pots in the galley all joined in a symphony of unfamiliar sounds. Water slapped rhythmically against the hull as our ship rocked in her mooring.

Reluctantly, I began to unpack. Thaddeus slipped from his bunk and rummaged for his tin soldiers.

"Can I set them up in here?" he asked.

"May I," I repeated automatically, and smiled at him. Sometimes my brother looked like an angel, with his shock of black hair so like Papa's, and his eyes the color of fog. "Best play with them in the day cabin out of my way, Tad. And mind you don't touch any of Papa's things!"

He nodded and, gathering up his toys, disappeared.

Removing everything but our winter clothes, which I planned to leave in our sea chests and stow in the space beneath our bunks, I set about the task at hand.

Suddenly, I heard a shriek from Thaddeus, followed by a splash.

Dropping a pile of Papa's shirts, I rushed into the day cabin.

"Tad!" I screamed in horror.

He had fallen from the stern window!

I climbed onto the sofa and leaned out. Below, my little brother splashed frantically. He looked up, his small face tight with panic, and opened his mouth to call to me.

He barely got the first syllable out before he swallowed a big gulp of seawater, slipped under, and began to thrash.

I screamed again, "Papa!" this time. Bending over, I fumbled with the buttons on my shoes. Fear cramped my fingers. Thaddeus was not a strong swimmer.

Before I could leap to his aid, however, I heard another splash. Leaning out the window once again, I saw a dark head bobbing in the water, just a few feet from my brother. Then a strong arm snaked out and grabbed him, lifting his head above the waves. There were shouts from the deck above, and someone threw down a rope. The man in the water hugged Thaddeus to him tightly. He was safe!

Barefoot, heart pounding, I raced up on deck.

"Thunder and lightning, Patience!" Papa bellowed, as Thaddeus and his rescuer were hauled aboard. "You were to keep a close eye on him!"

Dripping and coughing, Thaddeus flung himself at me while Papa reached out and grasped the shoulder of the tall black man who stood by his side. "I am much indebted to you, Chips," he said.

The man nodded mutely and padded away, leaving a trail of wet footprints in his wake.

"I didn't mean to fall," Thaddeus sobbed, clinging to me like a barnacle to a rock.

"Hush now, Tad, it's all right," I said soothingly. "You're safe."

Stricken with guilt, I hugged him close, patting him gently, and his sobs gradually receded into hiccups.

My guilt turned quickly to fury. Papa had no right to bring us here. Martha was right—a whaling ship was far too dangerous for children. Thaddeus could easily have drowned! My little brother was often a nuisance, but I loved him dearly, and my poor heart had been battered enough these past months without losing him, too. Glancing over his head, my eyes met Papa's. His face was as grim as my own, shuttered tight as a hatch battened against a rising gale.

"We'll discuss this later," he said. "Take your brother below and dry him off. And see if you can manage to keep him aboard this time."

Our midday meal was a subdued affair. There were six of us at the dinner table, Papa and Thaddeus and me, of course, and two other officers in addition to Cousin Jeremiah—Henry Chase, the *Morning Star*'s rotund, florid-faced second mate, and the spruce young third mate, John Macy. Slender as a cat's tail, he had a prominent Adam's apple and a reedy voice that cracked frequently, much to his embarrassment.

Thaddeus, chastened, ate in silence, while Papa, who was calmly discussing the prospects for wind and tide with Cousin Jeremiah and the others, ignored us both.

My stomach in knots, I could only pick at my chicken and dumplings. Here we were not even out of the harbor yet and already disaster had struck. Surely Papa would come to his senses and put us ashore!

Finally, Papa pushed his plate away and turned his attention to the two of us. His expression was stern.

"I suppose this is to be expected when one brings children aboard," he said.

I held my breath, hoping against hope that he had changed his mind.

There was a tapping on the skylight above, and we all looked up to see the face of Thaddeus's rescuer. He signaled to Papa, who nodded and stood up from the table.

Motioning for us to follow, he stepped into the day cabin.

"I've taken steps to ensure that it won't happen again," he said, pulling open the mullioned window. There, stretched across the opening, was a length of netting, the same sort our island fishermen used.

"I call it the Tad-Catcher," said Papa gruffly. "Spoils our looks, I suppose, but it's better than having my son bobbing like a cork in our wake."

October 12, 1835

Aunt Anne gave me this journal. It's very handsome, bound in red morocco leather with gilt edges. On the cover are stamped the words "The Voyage of Patience Goodspeed." Cousin Jeremiah gave Thaddeus and me each a set of whale stamps just like the ones he uses for the ship's log, and I have promised to keep a record of our voyage so that Aunt Anne can read about it when we return home.

Thaddeus is playing quietly on his bunk with his tin soldiers. He has been as good as gold since his accident this morning. As it appears we are not going to be put ashore after all, I finished unpacking, and made up our bunks with Mama's bright patchwork quilts. When Papa came down a few minutes ago to inspect he pronounced everything "shipshape and Bristol fashion." I don't know what "Bristol fashion" means, but it must be something good, as he obviously approves.

I hear Papa calling us now, so I must close.

—P.

Thaddeus and I emerged from the companionway to find the deck abuzz with activity. Papa was bawling orders at the crew in the Cape Horn voice we knew all too well.

"Haul lively, men! Bear a hand there, and hoist the mainsail—handsomely, now, handsomely!"

We crossed to where he was standing by the mizzenmast and watched, Thaddeus openmouthed with excitement, as several of the crew clambered up the ratlines into the rigging to loose the canvas sails, while others hauled on the halyards below. Forward, more men strained at the windlass as they heaved up the *Morning Star*'s anchor to the words of a familiar shanty:

> Oh, Cape Cod girls ain't got no combs,
> Heave away! Heave away!
> They comb their hair with codfish bones,
> Heave away! Heave away!
> Heave away, my bully, bully boys, heave away,
> heave away!
> Heave away, now won't you make some noise;
> We are bound for Australia!

As our ship slowly caught the breeze and slipped away from her mooring, the good smell of chowder wafted from the galley behind us. I had hardly eaten anything at dinner, and my stomach growled noisily.

Thaddeus and I ran back to the taffrail as we pulled away from the mouth of the harbor to watch as the wharves, the town, and all that was familiar, receded in our wake. After a while, Papa joined us.

"Bid farewell to Nantucket, children, you won't be seeing her until many a tide has turned," he said.

My eyes filled with tears at his words and I felt a sudden twinge of panic. There was no turning back now. My fate was sealed, and any lingering hopes I might have cherished of staying ashore and continuing my studies with Miss Mitchell were well and truly dashed. I was going to sea whether I liked it or not.

We were moving away from the shoreline's sheltered waters now, and as the *Morning Star*'s sails caught the stronger breezes of the open sea her deck began to spring beneath my feet like a live thing, with a rhythmic rise and fall that made me slightly giddy.

Soon we cleared Great Point and as we did, a tall, fair-haired sailor struck up a bittersweet tune of farewell on his fiddle. I gazed past our wake, which spooled out behind us like a foamy bridal veil, to where our small island was fast receding in the distance, held close in the horizon's embrace.

"Good-bye, Nantucket," I called softly, as the tears finally splashed down over my cheeks. "Good-bye, Mama."

Later, at supper, Thaddeus's head began to bob sleepily, until he was in peril of falling face first into his chowder bowl.

"Too much excitement for one day," said Cousin Jeremiah with a wink at me.

"Indeed," added Papa wryly.

I excused myself from the table and led my little brother toward our stateroom.

"Patience?" Thaddeus asked, as I tucked him into his bunk.

"Yes?"

"Do you think Mama can see us? Do you think she knows that we are at sea?"

I considered his question carefully. I don't believe in ghosts, nor do I think that the dead gather at some heavenly vantage point from which they can peer down at us. Still, "I think she knows," I replied.

I smoothed his hair back from his forehead gently then, like Mama used to do, and he smiled up at me and closed his eyes.

My own eyelids were drooping, so after bidding him good night I undressed and crept quietly into my own bunk. Blowing out the whale-oil lamp, I pulled the quilt up under my chin.

I lay there in the dark, listening to the low murmur of voices from the main cabin where Papa and the officers lingered at the table, and wondered whether I would ever grow accustomed to the strange noises and movements of the ship. This was much different than sleeping in my room at home, where the only sound was the wind in the trees outside my window. The *Morning Star* creaked and groaned as she plowed forward through the waves, rocking to and fro, and as I listened to the distant thumps and calls of the men on deck—and even the gentle snoring that emerged from Thaddeus's bunk above me—I felt that sleep would be impossible.

I was wrong, however. Exhaustion finally won out, and I, too, closed my eyes and drifted off to sleep.

Four

It's now we're out to sea my boys,
The wind comes on to blow;
One half the watch is sick on deck,
The other half sick below.

—*Blow Ye Winds*

October 15, 1835

Three days outward bound and I have yet to set foot on deck since we weighed anchor. Much to our shame, Thaddeus and I have been confined to our bunks with Neptune's revenge, our stomachs lurching with each roll of the ship.

Papa laughs and calls us lubbers, and says it will soon pass. Half the crew are equally afflicted, he says. We are all in the same boat, he says, slapping his leg and laughing again at the joke he has made.

A feeble one, as I find nothing laughable about our condition. I have barely the strength to hold my pen, but am determined to keep my promise and put down on record all my experiences—even this vile seasickness.

The ship pitches sideways and I grab for the

*bucket again, glaring at Papa, certain that I will
expire here in this cabin. Won't he be sorry then!*
—*P.*

Papa was right, as it happened. This morning Thaddeus and I awoke good as new, the only pains in our bellies those of hunger. Sprigg, our steward, served us an enormous breakfast and we ate every bite.

Much to our dismay, in the wake of the accident we had been placed in Sprigg's care for the duration of the voyage. The steward was no more pleased with this arrangement than we were, and spent most of the breakfast hour scowling and muttering darkly to himself. Wizened as a dried apple, with a gray pigtail, spectacles, and a voice like a rusty hinge, a more disagreeable old sea dog than Pardon Sprigg would be difficult to find, though Papa said his temperament was due to his disappointment in life. Sprigg was once a harpooneer, he told us, but his eyes began to fail him a few years ago and now he wouldn't recognize a whale if one swam up and bit him in the behind. Sprigg didn't take kindly to being made one of the "idlers"—what the crew called the cook, cooper or barrelmaker, carpenter, and steward, who stand no night watches on deck, nor lower away into the whaleboats when our quarry is sighted—but it was either that or leave the sea altogether. And if Papa was the undisputed monarch of our shipboard kingdom, Sprigg was if nothing else a loyal subject, no more disposed to being landlocked than he was to having us added to his duties, which certainly did not improve his humor.

Terrified that we would get into some mischief and bring the wrath of Papa down upon his head, Sprigg made us sit at the table for a full hour while he cleared away the breakfast dishes and tidied both the main cabin and the pantry. Fairly prostrate with boredom, Thaddeus and I made goggle eyes at each other behind his back, until Papa finally came below and gave us—and the peevish steward—a reprieve.

"I'll take the children now, Sprigg, you may go about your other duties," he said.

"Aye, sir," said a visibly grateful Sprigg, who disappeared into the pantry with more speed than I'd have given his aged legs credit for.

Thaddeus and I tottered up on deck after Papa, still a little wobbly from our bout of seasickness.

"Mind you keep a weather eye on your brother, now, Patience," said Papa, "and stay aft here where you won't get in the way."

I glared at him. "Why did you drag us along, then, if you're so worried that we'll be in the way?" I muttered.

Papa looked at me sharply, seemed on the point of saying something more, then spun on his heel and stalked forward to where the officers were gathered.

The sun was painfully bright after my days of confinement below, and I moved into the shade of the afterhouse and stood at the taffrail, breathing deeply the clean, salt-sharp air. The *Morning Star*'s wake spun out behind us like a line of fresh washing flapping in the breeze, a steady curl of white foam against the deep, deep blue of the sea.

We were completely alone on the water, with nary a speck of land in sight. Blue sky and blue sea stretched away to every point on the compass, with only the faintest of lines to distinguish where they joined at the horizon.

There was a fine breeze, too, and moving forward again, I braced myself against the skylight and looked upwards to where the sails stretched taut, full-bellied before the wind. The rigging hummed with each strong gust, and in spite of my black mood I felt a rush of exhilaration as we surged through the water and the deck swayed beneath my feet.

My stomach gave a sudden lurch as I looked around me and realized that Thaddeus was nowhere to be seen. Before concern could blossom into full-blown panic, however, his head popped out from behind the mizzenmast.

"Patience!" he cried happily. "Come and see what Chips has made for me!"

I followed him past the deckhouse, hesitating at the line that Papa had had painted across the deck. Forward of this line we were not to go under any circumstances, he had informed us at breakfast, unless we were invited.

"Captain's given permission, miss," Chips called, seeing my hesitation.

I followed Thaddeus to the worktable beneath the mainmast that is Chips's kingdom. His name wasn't really Chips, Cousin Jeremiah had told us, it was William Thomas, but it was tradition at sea to call the ship's carpenter "Chips"—for the curls of wood and sawdust shavings that characterized his trade, I supposed.

Thaddeus stopped in front of a small, boy-size boat that was lying on the deck.

"I thought it might cheer him up, what with the seasickness and all," the tall dark man said with a shy smile.

I prodded my brother and nodded significantly in Chips's direction.

"Thankee, sir, for the fine gift," Thaddeus said dutifully, with a worshipful glance at the carpenter.

Proper etiquette thus observed, Chips hoisted the little boat onto his shoulder and carried it back to the deckhouse. Now that we were under way, Papa said that he would use his day cabin for an office and had turned the small shed over to Thaddeus and me. It would be a safe place for us to play and do our lessons, he said. Inside, there was a table bolted to the wall, a bench, and a low, short bunk that would serve as a sofa, whose cushions lifted to reveal a storage locker beneath for toys, books, blankets, and the like.

"All hands on deck!" shouted Cousin Jeremiah, and I peeked forward curiously as the men gathered obediently by the mainmast.

I glanced at Thaddeus, who was playing with his new boat, happy as a clam at high tide, and wondered if it were safe to venture further forward. Papa was bound to notice if I stepped over the painted line, however, and it wouldn't do to vex him again so soon, much as I dearly longed to get a closer look at the buzz of activity.

There must be a better vantage point, I thought. I looked up. Papa had banned us from the ratlines, the ladderlike ropes that led up into the rigging, but he hadn't said anything about not climbing elsewhere. I contemplated the spare whaleboat that rested atop the midship shelter, a broad platform of planks extending forward from the deck house, from which sprouted pegs for buckets and racks that bristled with harpoons and lances and other sharp implements of the whaling trade.

Grabbing a bucket, I turned it over and set it on

the deck. I glanced around, but no one was paying me the slightest bit of attention. Stepping onto it, I managed to clamber onto the roof of the deckhouse, and from there picked my way over a pile of oars and pulled myself up onto the overturned whaleboat.

Papa was standing on the main hatch, his back turned toward me. So was Sprigg's, fortunately.

"Patience, can I come up too?" My little brother had discovered my hiding place.

"Oh very well," I replied crossly, and reached down to haul him up. "And it's *may* I, not *can* I."

We surveyed the crew, and I gasped in alarm as I recognized the two ruffians from the Spouter Tavern. Beefy wharfrats both, they lounged insolently against the waist of the *Morning Star,* the one called Binyon picking his teeth with a wicked-looking knife.

"Quick, Thaddeus, get down!" I whispered urgently. "Don't let them see you!"

My brother ducked his head obediently, and we slid off the overturned whaleboat and flattened ourselves onto the roof. Quietly, I reached over the edge, and grabbing first one bucket, and then another, slowly, carefully pulled them up and placed them in front of us. Not the most artful concealment, but it would have to do. I didn't want to risk climbing back down onto the deck, for fear we might knock something over and attract attention.

"Do you think they saw me?" asked Thaddeus anxiously.

I put my arm around his shoulders and gave him a reassuring squeeze. "Not at all, Tad. Anyway, they were none too steady on their feet that day, as I recall, and I doubt they have any memory of our meeting."

He relaxed a bit at this, and we peered around the edges of the buckets at the rest of the crew. There were well over a dozen of them, a ragtag assortment of age, size, and color. Several looked fairly young—one in particular, a red-headed lad with a broad, honest face whose greenish pallor revealed a lingering discomfort with life at sea, could only have been a few years older than me. At breakfast earlier, Cousin Jeremiah had described the men as "polyglot"—which meant many-tongued, he told Thaddeus and me.

"Besides Nantucket men, the *Morning Star*'s crew hails from New York and Ohio, from England and Ireland, Germany, Sweden, Italy—why, there are even a pair of brothers from the Sandwich Islands. 'Kanakas' we call them."

I spotted the Kanakas right away, standing side by side, their bare arms covered with rather alarming-looking tattoos. They were nearly as dark skinned as Chips, who was one of the many free blacks who resided on our island, which with its Quaker influence harbored a strong antislavery sentiment. Next to Chips stood Owen Gardiner, our cooper, and beside him were Sprigg and the cook. The officers were massed behind Papa, who began to speak.

"Well, men," Papa said sternly, looking very fine in his blue coat and stovepipe hat, "you've come a-whaling, and a-whaling you shall go. We are setting out on this voyage for one reason and one reason only. To get a cargo of oil. If you pull your weight and obey orders, we'll succeed, and all return home the richer for it."

He thrust his hands behind his back and leaned forward. I couldn't see his face from here, but by the tone of his voice I knew that his eyebrows were lowered into their storm warning position.

"I won't stand slackers or grumblers, and I won't stand for disobedience or disrespect to me or the officers," he said, with a sharp glance at Binyon, who straightened up and affixed a meek expression to his face. "There'll be no fighting, no skylarking, and no sleeping on watches."

Papa continued on in this fashion for a bit, laying down the law, then turned to the business of whale hunting.

"You will each take a turn at the masthead lookout, and you must sing out lively when you spot a whale," he said. "If you see a spout, sing out, 'There she blows!' If land, shout 'Land ho!' and if another ship, 'Sail ho!'"

Papa held up a shiny silver dollar. It glittered in the bright morning sunlight, drawing every eye like a magnet.

"This goes to the lucky man who spies our first whale," he said, as Cousin Jeremiah passed him a hammer and nail. Papa stepped down from the hatch and, turning, strode ceremoniously to the mainmast. Thaddeus and I ducked our heads again and held our breath, hoping he wouldn't spot us. With a few loud whacks, he nailed the silver dollar to the wood. "Keep a weather eye out now, men, and good luck to you. Mr. Folger, let the officers choose the watches and boat crews."

With that, Papa strode aft, passing directly beneath us and disappearing down the companionway.

We returned our attention forward to where the mates were dividing the men into two groups. Cousin Jeremiah had explained this process to us at breakfast, using pieces of toast to serve as the *Morning Star*'s four whaleboats.

"Your Papa's boat hangs off the starboard davits— that pair of curved wooden posts that extend out over the side of our ship," he said. "Directly opposite, on the larboard or port side, is my boat. In front of it is the waistboat, which belongs to Mr. Chase"—

the second mate hoisted his coffee cup in a mock salute—"and Mr. Macy's boat hangs off the port bow. The men will be divided into watches, as well as into crews to man the whaleboats."

From where we were seated now, it all became clear. After the men had been divided into two groups, Cousin Jeremiah moved one group to the starboard side of the ship.

"You men constitute the starboard watch," he announced. "Mr. Chase is your watch officer. You others"—he turned to face the group on his left—"are the port watch, under Mr. Macy."

"What's a watch, Patience?" Thaddeus whispered, mystified. "Is he talking about Papa's pocket watch?"

I had to smile at this. "No, Tad. A watch at sea means something entirely different. It's the period of time during which the men are on duty. The port and starboard watches will take turns all day and night, one watch working while the other rests."

My little brother nodded his head, his brow puckered as he absorbed this information.

"Mr. Chase, Mr. Macy, you may split the men into boat crews," Cousin Jeremiah said.

I glanced over at the spare whaleboat beside us. It seemed a frail craft, little more than a canoe, really. To think of taking it out on the open sea after a whale!

Cousin Jeremiah started aft toward us. He paused briefly beneath the midship shelter and cleared his throat.

"You'd best come down from there before Sprigg sees you," he said softly. "And put those buckets back where you found them."

Reluctantly, we climbed down. Cousin Jeremiah winked conspiratorially, and said he'd try and gain permission for us to watch the morning's training from behind the steerage hatch.

"That's all right, Cousin Jeremiah," I said hastily. "We can watch from the deckhouse."

I didn't add that we'd be safer there from prying eyes, too. Despite my assurances to Thaddeus, I didn't want to risk jogging the memory of Binyon and his companion.

The deckhouse wasn't a perfect vantage point, but still, we were able to see enough as Papa and the other officers spent the next few hours breaking in the new hands.

Learning to reef and steer, to trim the sails smartly when told to and to coil each line neatly and put it in its proper place was clearly no easy task for the "greenies," as Papa and Cousin Jeremiah called those with no experience at sea, and soon Papa was hollering at the top of his voice, peppering his orders with "thunder and lightning" and "blast" and the rest of his favorite cuss words, and even adding a few I had never heard before.

"I can tie knots better than that red-haired fellow over there," said Thaddeus, nudging me.

"I believe you're right," I replied, watching as the boy fumbled with the end of a rope, and finally threw it down in frustration.

Papa shook his head in disgust, and the fellow's more able shipmates—led by Binyon, I noted—began to make sport of him, calling him "hayseed" and "bumpkin" until he was close to tears.

A few minutes later, when he caught his foot in a line and he was accidentally hauled upward along with the mainsail, the whole crew exploded with laughter. He dangled upside down some ten feet above deck for a minute, until the cook rang the bell for dinner and Cousin Jeremiah came to his rescue.

After he was safely disentangled, the red-haired boy headed toward the fo'c'sle, a dejected look on his face.

"Young Firetop there is as green as my Aunt Lily's lettuce patch," said Binyon, and another shout of laughter went up as his hapless prey's face turned bright pink. He nudged his companion. "Ent that right, Todd?"

The other sailor nodded. "Green as a pond frog," he echoed.

"Leave him be now, boys," said the tall, fair-haired

sailor who had serenaded our departure, a Swede I'd heard the men call Long Tom.

Binyon swiveled around. "Who are you to tell us when to leave off?" he said belligerently.

"You've had your fun," said Long Tom evenly. "Why don't you go cool off before dinner."

"We'll cool off when we're ready to cool off," Binyon replied, taking a step toward him.

Chips, who had been busy at his work table, straightened up and nodded at Owen Gardiner, the cooper. Moving quietly, they closed in behind Long Tom, and the three of them stood facing Binyon and Todd.

"Is there going to be a fight, Patience?" asked Thaddeus in a nervous voice.

"Hush, Tad," I said, wishing fervently that we were belowdecks.

Cousin Jeremiah suddenly materialized. "Is there a problem, gentlemen?" he asked calmly. "You heard the captain, there's to be no brawling on this ship, and I assure you that anyone I catch at it will be dealt with most severely."

With a defiant jerk of his chin at Long Tom, Binyon swaggered off, trailing Todd behind him.

"Well, don't just stand there like ninnies, didn't you hear the dinner bell?" said Sprigg in an exasperated voice, coming up behind us as the rest of the men dispersed. Grabbing us both by our ears, he marched us below.

The noon meal was a lively affair. Cousin Jeremiah said nothing of the disagreement on deck, and, with appetites sharpened by the fine weather, we all tucked into our plates of stew with gusto. Papa and the officers took great delight in recounting the morning's misadventures in general, and those of the red-haired boy, whose name we were told was Charlie Fishback, in particular.

"Have you ever seen such a lubber?" Papa asked. "Fresh off the farm—I'd wager the only line he's ever held had a cow at the other end!"

"Clumsy as a hog on ice," agreed Mr. Chase.

Cousin Jeremiah winked at Thaddeus and added, "I declare I saw a piece of hay still stuck behind one of his ears!"

A roar of laughter went up around the table, and though I felt sorry for the poor boy, even I had to giggle at that. Only our cook didn't laugh. His name was Obadiah Glumly, and never had there lived a man so aptly named. His face was set in a perpetually mournful expression, which set me to wondering whether people lived up to the names their parents chose for them. But I quickly discarded the thought, for I was certainly the most impatient creature imaginable.

In fact, Mama used to tell me that she named me

Patience because she could tell the minute I was born it was a virtue of which she was going to be greatly in need.

Glum, as everyone called him, was nothing like what I thought a cook should be. Cooks should be like Martha, fat and cheerful and fond of the meals they provide. Glum was forlorn and cadaverous, and if he ever swallowed a bite of food, I don't think anyone had caught him at it yet. When he called us to dinner, you would swear he was announcing a funeral, so remarkably solemn was his tone.

Bald as an egg and with not an ounce of spare flesh on his tall, storklike frame, he lingered on the companionway stairs at mealtimes, arms folded across his narrow chest, and watched dolefully as each forkful of food progressed from the plate to our mouths. It was enough to spoil anyone's appetite, although I seemed to be the only one who noticed. Everyone else ignored him.

At dinner, I learned that we were still at least a week's sailing from the Azores, or Western Islands off Portugal, where we would put in at Fayal for fresh supplies and fill out our complement of experienced hands. Papa said the Portuguese islanders were well known for their seamanship, and he was eager to round out our crew before we reached Cape Horn.

October 16, 1835

Cape Horn! The very words fill me with dread. To anyone raised on Nantucket they are synonymous with danger and death.

"The graveyard of the sea," sailors call it, and from childhood I have heard hair-raising tales of passages round that icy, forsaken bit of land that juts down from South America like the tip of a harpoon. Weather so cold that even in summer blankets freeze solid. Treacherous winds that howl down from the Andes and raise waves so high they look like mountains, and can swallow a ship twice the size of a whaler. Even though Papa says this is the most favorable time of year to make the passage, I find myself growing more anxious with every day that brings us closer to it, and with the added discovery of Binyon and Todd aboard, I am altogether uneasy.

—P.

Five

It was a fine ship with prime captain and crew,
Surpassed by none and equaled by few.
With courage undaunted by oars and by sail,
So nimble we chased the spermaceti whale.

—The Cruise of the Dove

Though the *Morning Star* hardly felt like home, our days quickly settled into a routine as Thaddeus and I caught the rhythm of shipboard life.

Each morning we were awakened at dawn to the sound of the decks being scrubbed. Papa was a stickler for cleanliness. "A tidy ship is a happy ship," he told us.

Be that as it may, I did not feel particularly happy, nor had I forgiven Papa for forcing me to accompany him on this voyage. I still sorely missed Nantucket, my mathematical studies (though I was forging ahead a bit on my own with the texts Miss Mitchell had provided me), and even Martha.

Too, I was growing weary of Papa's constant harping about how a ship's crew was like a family. "Stronger together than when we work alone," he would often say. "Each one has his particular abilities, and if everyone does his duty, we'll weather every storm and danger safely."

Empty words, as far as I was concerned. How cruel of the fates to take Mama, who had loved us so, and leave us with Papa, who treated us as strangers despite all his fine talk about family!

How little he really knew about my brother and me. Mama had always taken a keen interest in everything that we did, but Papa seemed altogether indifferent. He had yet to so much as glance at my schoolwork, while Cousin Jeremiah, on the other hand, frequently popped by to look over my shoulder.

"Trigonometry!" he would say with a low whistle, watching as I wrestled with a particularly thorny algorithm and offering encouragement when I needed help making sense of all the sines and cosines, tangents and cotangents. Cousin Jeremiah was family too, of course, but still, it was Papa's approval for which I secretly yearned.

His moods shifted as unpredictably as the weather, and his manner with me was rigidly formal—although I had to admit my own fault in that regard, as I mulishly continued to rebuff his intermittent attempts to make peace. As for Thaddeus, well, Papa didn't seem to fathom what to do with Thaddeus. My little brother regarded him with a mixture of shyness and awe, and was as skittish around him as a spring colt.

None of this escaped the notice of Cousin

Jeremiah, who took me aside one afternoon while Papa was in his day cabin.

"Your father's not an easy man with words, Cousin Patience," he said awkwardly, "and I gather that you're not entirely delighted to be here aboard the *Morning Star*. But I do know that you and your brother are very dear to him, something that you will perhaps see for yourself in time."

My cheeks flamed with embarrassment. I was ashamed that Cousin Jeremiah thought me a sulky miss, and longed to explain the reasons for my resentment, but pride bridled my tongue.

For Cousin Jeremiah's sake, if not Papa's—I had no intention of allowing him to bend me to his will, after all—I tried to put on a more cheerful face. After breakfast each day I dutifully attended to my chores, making up our bunks and tidying our cabin under the watchful eye of Sprigg. Then Thaddeus and I would do our lessons at the table, or, if Sprigg was in a particularly good humor, in the day cabin. Later in the morning, if the weather was fine, we were allowed up on deck to play—or Thaddeus played, at least, while I watched the crew as they practiced lowering the whaleboats and chasing after the barrels Papa tossed overboard as dummy whales. Sometimes I sat on the sofa in the deckhouse and read.

Rarely were we out of range of Sprigg, however. If I thought Martha was a trial and a tribulation, Pardon Sprigg was infinitely worse. Fussy as a broody hen, he hovered over us morning, noon, and night, continually grumbling to himself about being over-worked and underappreciated. He might have been nearsighted, but there was nothing wrong with his hearing, and woe betide the child in his care who uttered a word of complaint or snickered at him behind his back. He carried a thimble in his front pocket, and both Thaddeus and I had been brought up short on numerous occasions by a thump on the head when we stepped out of line.

So far we had managed to avoid Binyon and Todd (whom Thaddeus and I called "Bunion" and "Toad" behind their backs). Not that we needed to take such pains, it seemed. If they noticed us at all, they gave no indication that they remembered our encounter on the Nantucket wharf.

What we had not been able to manage was to climb up again atop the spare whaleboat, which was a shame as it afforded by far the best view of the goings-on aboard the *Morning Star.* Not that the goings-on had been all that lively of late.

October 20, 1835

Eight days out and still no whales. Papa is grow-ing restless. By his reckoning, we should arrive in Fayal before another fortnight has passed, just in time for my birthday. Papa would dearly love to take at least one whale by then.

The silver dollar still gleams from the mainmast, and all the men are in the habit now of touching it as they pass, for luck. This morning, Sprigg allowed us forward with him to feed the chickens and pigs, and Tad and I touched it too.

—*P.*

P.S. Speaking of pigs, the red-haired farmboy must be homesick as well as seasick, as he crept aft last night into the hold and was found curled up asleep with them in the pen this morning.

While our days proceeded at a leisurely pace, those of the crew were vastly different. They worked around the clock keeping the *Morning Star* on her course and practicing in the whaleboats.

I was very eager to see their quarters forward in the fo'c'sle, but that of course was expressly forbidden. Thaddeus managed to slip down once when Binyon and Todd were safely away drilling in the whaleboats, but was quickly fished out by Sprigg and roundly thumped for his trouble. He told me that it was dark and smoky, and smelled of stale fish and old boots. The men were packed into narrow bunks like sardines, he said.

Our officers were more fortunate. Cousin Jeremiah had a stateroom to himself off the main cabin. It was tiny, with just enough room for his bunk, a sea chest, and a small desk at which he kept the official ship's log. The second and third mates bunked together in a nearly identical stateroom across from him, while Sprigg, Glum, Chips, and the cooper bunked amidships in steerage with the harpooneers.

Thaddeus and I soon learned the names of the equipment used aboard the *Morning Star*, from the binnacle, which stood forward of the helm and housed the compass, to the various tools of the whaling trade, the harpoons and blubber gaffs and mincing knives, and the half-dozen different cutting spades the men would use to butcher the whales once we caught them.

Thaddeus, of course, was fondest of the more barbarous implements, and had taken to standing in his little boat with a wooden spoon pilfered from Glum, spearing imaginary whales. I, on the other hand, was drawn to the navigational instruments, the fine brass chronometer in its wooden box and the sextants and charts and dividers that Papa and Cousin Jeremiah used to fix our position each day and plot our course.

I loved to watch as they took the noon sight with their sextants, and my heart leaped when I observed Mr. Chase and Mr. Macy struggling with their navigational equations. I knew that my own mathematical skills were already equal to—or better than—theirs. But when I asked Papa if he would teach me to navigate, he only laughed.

"What use would you find for that, once you are ashore again?" he asked.

Stung, I bit back an insolent retort. Clearly, Papa was either too proud or too busy to take an interest in me, and even if he did, it was evident there were bounds to his sentiment about members of a ship's crew and their "abilities." I was merely a lowly subject in our kingdom at sea.

Thaddeus, meanwhile, divided up his toy soldiers into watches, and it was very comical to hear him mimicking Papa and the mates as he ordered them around his little ship in tiny whaleboats that Chips and other members of the crew had carved for him. He was very much the pet of the *Morning Star* by now, and had taken to shadowing Chips when Sprigg gave him permission. The carpenter had made him his own little toolbox, and he bustled about industriously pounding nails into scraps of wood.

I envied Thaddeus his illusion of usefulness. Aside from tutoring him, keeping up with my own lessons and tidying our cabin each morning, I had no role aboard ship to speak of and found to my surprise that I was growing bored. Grudgingly, I approached Papa and asked if I could be of help to him in any way—secretly hoping, of course, that if he wouldn't teach me to navigate, he would at least see fit to allow me to assist him with the charts, or with his logbook.

October 22, 1835

So much for my desire to be of use. Papa has now assigned us official duties, and while Thaddeus is to care for the livestock—feeding the pigs in the hold and the chickens we keep penned up beneath Chips's work table, collecting eggs, and milking Daisy, our goat—I have been foisted upon the cook.

Glum's dislike for me hovers in the galley like a black cloud, and he gives me the vilest of chores—picking weevils from the ship's biscuits, scrubbing slush from the pots with rough bits of shark hide, peeling endless mounds of potatoes. Nothing I do pleases him, and he plagues me until I want to smack him on his smug, bald head with a haddock.

Still, it is pleasant to be in a kitchen again, even a small, cramped galley such as this. Although I am a sorry laggard in most of the domestic arts—stitchery of any sort is beyond me, and Mama always declared that I was far too tol-

erant of dust—still, I have ever felt at home in the kitchen. Likely because I enjoy eating so much.

I seem to have a modest gift for baking, and there were smiles all around today when I appeared with a platter piled high with hot biscuits. We have no buttermilk aboard the Morning Star, *of course, so I tried Mama's old trick of souring milk with vinegar. Daisy provided the milk, and Glum, reluctantly, the vinegar. It seems to have done the trick, as there were no complaints, and even the biscuits I left for Glum as a peace offering disappeared without so much as a crumb, though knowing him he probably fired them over the taffrail when no one was looking.*

—P.

Six

It's a whale, oh a whale, and a whalefish, he cries,
And he blows at every span, brave boys,
And he blows at every span.

—The Whalefish Song

"Blows! She blows!"

My voice came out in a high squeak. I swatted frantically at the wet laundry that flapped in my face—since Papa assigned us duties, Sprigg had suddenly felt free to add to my chores, and I was hanging up freshly washed bed linen and undergarments—and squinted at the small cloud on the horizon behind us. Yes, it was most definitely a spout!

I cupped my hands around my mouth and shouted again, louder this time, "There she blows!" and in my excitement promptly fell off the overturned bucket on which I had been standing to reach the clothesline. I had quite got my sea legs now, and no longer staggered about the deck like a drunkard every time the ship pitched and rolled, but balancing on a makeshift stool in a lively sea was another trick altogether.

Binyon was skylarking at the masthead, pulling faces at Todd below instead of scanning the sea for whales.

Cousin Jeremiah was at the helm, engrossed in teaching Charlie Fishback, the red-haired boy, to steer, else he would have seen and given him old Harry for sure.

My cries and the clatter of the bucket drew their attention, however.

"She blows!" I hollered for the third time, mortified to be drawing attention to the wet petticoats and pantaloons that dangled behind me but gesturing wildly in their direction nonetheless.

Cousin Jeremiah looked puzzled for a moment, then grinned broadly and, as the others took up the cry, called for Papa, who came running up from below with his spyglass in his hand.

"Where away?" he shouted.

Cousin Jeremiah pointed to me, I pointed behind us, and Binyon, who looked quite indignant at the fact that I, and not he, had spotted the whale, saw a chance to redeem himself and roared, "Off the starboard quarter, sir!"

"Patience, my girl, I should send you aloft instead of these lubbers," cried Papa in a jubilant tone. "Unless I'm mistaken, there are at least two whales out there. You're a Goodspeed through and through!"

I beamed at the unaccustomed praise.

"Call all hands!" he thundered. "Tumble up, men, and stand by to clew up the foretopgallant sail! Hard down on the wheel and haul aback the main yard! Bear a hand now!"

The watch sprang to do his bidding, and as word of the whale spread to the fo'c'sle, the rest of the crew scrambled up on deck to see this long-awaited sight.

Tipping his hat in my direction, Papa roared, "Well, men, shown up by a slip of a girl! Patience, you shall have your reward."

And with that he strode to the mainmast and pried off the silver dollar. Cousin Jeremiah swept me forward amidst the cheers of the assembled crew, and Papa handed it to me with a ceremonial flourish.

"I knew you'd bring good luck to the *Morning Star*," Cousin Jeremiah said, clasping my hand and wringing it heartily.

Out of the corner of my eye I saw Binyon, who had clambered down from the masthead to join the throng, regarding me sourly. He leaned over and whispered something to Todd, who peered at me with a frown. I ducked my head to avoid their gaze.

Still grinning from ear to ear, Papa turned to the men. "Get your tubs in your boats, men, and stand by all to lower!"

"Aye, sir," came the reply, as the crew hastened to fetch the wooden tubs containing the neatly coiled line that would soon, if all went well, fasten a whaleboat to its quarry.

Sprigg appeared trailing Thaddeus in his wake and hustled us out of harm's way into the deckhouse, where we hopped up on the sofa and peered through the windows to watch the activity as best we could. We would remain behind, of course, with the idlers, who always stayed aboard as shipkeepers in the captain's absence.

Papa's whaleboat was the first to lower away, and as soon as it hit the water he and the crew climbed down into their places.

Papa took his seat in the stern, opposite Big John, the tall Kanaka whom he had chosen for his harpooneer. They pushed away from the ship and the men began to row, the boat moving slowly at first, then gathering speed. Papa's face was alight with excitement, and his voice carried back toward us as he urged his men forward.

"Put your backs into it, men!" he called. "Pull! This is what you've come for!"

Cousin Jeremiah's boat was being lowered now, and I couldn't help but notice the anxious expression on the red-haired boy's face.

"A dead whale or a stove boat, eh, Charlie?" called Binyon.

Todd nudged him in the ribs. "Can I have your tobacco if you're swallowed up like old Jonah?"

There were shouts of laughter at this, and the boy's face turned bright pink. He glanced in my direction, and I gave him an encouraging smile. Then he was gone, over the side with the rest of the men to follow Papa.

After two of the whaleboats were away, Chips, Glum, Sprigg, and the cooper lined up at the taffrail to watch the proceedings. The *Morning Star,* which had been hove to, lay peacefully in the water, sails all aback and rolling with the swell. It seemed unnaturally quiet all of a sudden, and I realized with a sinking heart that Thaddeus was nowhere in sight.

I looked around wildly. Could he have stowed away on one of the boats?

No sooner had this unlikely possibility occurred to me than a scuffling noise from above caught my attention, and I looked up just in time to see Thaddeus scramble up the ratlines into the mainmast rigging.

"Come back down here at once!" I whispered as loudly as I dared, for Sprigg was only a few feet away.

"I won't!" he whispered back. "I can't see a thing from down there!"

He had a point. Confined to the deckhouse, we had as much chance of seeing the whalehunt as did the barnacles on the bottom of the ship.

I glanced in Sprigg's direction. He and his companions appeared to have forgotten us, so riveted were they to the sight of the slender whaleboats making their way toward the distant prey.

With a sigh I deposited the silver dollar—which I had been clutching in my hand since Papa gave it to me—in my pinafore pocket, hiked up my skirt and petticoat and tucked them into my pantaloons, then swung myself as quietly as I could into the rigging. We'd be thumped for sure if Sprigg caught us.

The hands made it look easy, but climbing aloft proved hard work. I fastened my gaze on my brother's feet and made my way carefully upward, step by step and hand over hand. Cautiously, I leaned out backward to maneuver my way around the top, and for the first time dared to look down. Instantly I wished I hadn't. The deck was very far away. Swallowing hard, I continued up toward the masthead, which swayed dizzyingly with each roll of the ship. Finally, panting, I reached the masthead, and clamored up to grip the canvas-padded edge of the iron masthoop that encircled us. Careful not to look down again, I scanned the horizon for Papa.

"There they are, Patience!" cried Thaddeus, nudging me. "Papa's boat is still in the lead!"

The distance between his whaleboat and the whale was closing swiftly. Thaddeus passed me his spyglass, and I watched the men straining at their oars. Big John was poised at the front of the boat, his harpoon resting on his shoulder. As the boat drew abreast of the whale, he tensed, then raised it over his head and, after standing perfectly motionless for a long moment, flung it forward with a sudden, powerful thrust.

"He hit it! He hit it!" cheered Thaddeus.

The men in Papa's boat began backing frantically away from the whale as it lurched from side to side, agitated by the harpoon. Then, with a flick of its broad tail, it disappeared beneath the surface of the sea.

"It's diving," said Thaddeus.

It was thrilling to finally see firsthand the hunt of which I had heretofore only heard tell, and I clutched my brother's hand. We could see the line whipping out of the tub, unspooling swiftly as the whale dove deeper and deeper. A thin trail of smoke arose from the friction this caused, and the men doused the tub with buckets of water to keep it from igniting.

My heart was racing nearly as fast as the line now, for I knew from the tales I had heard since childhood that if the whale kept diving, he could pull the boat under—and if he surfaced directly under the boat, it would be smashed to pieces.

"There he is again, Patience!"

I swung the spyglass in the direction Thaddeus was pointing and allowed myself to breathe easier. The whale had surfaced quite a distance away, and now it began swimming forward. Towed along in its wake, the whaleboat began moving forward too, and the men shipped their oars as both picked up speed.

The whale made a broad turn, and was now heading directly toward the *Morning Star.*

"He's coming this way," said Thaddeus, with less enthusiasm.

Fear welled up in me. Like every child on Nantucket, we had heard of the terrible voyage of the *Essex*. It had happened a few years before I was born, and was still spoken of on our island in hushed voices. Two thousand miles off the coast of South America, a whale turned on the *Essex* and rammed her—not once, but twice. Her side stove in, she quickly sank, and the men drifted for weeks in their whaleboats. In the end, some of them, including the captain, resorted to the unspeakable—surviving on the flesh of their companions. After he was rescued Captain Pollard gave up the sea to become a watchman, and now wandered the streets of Nantucket each night, haunted by his memories.

"Don't be frightened, Thaddeus," I said, though I myself was far from calm. "Papa knows what he's doing."

The whaleboat was skimming over the water at a tremendous speed now, and I could see the faces of Papa's crew. Some were holding on like grim death; others, like Doyle, the Irishman, and Long Tom were whooping with the thrill of what whalemen call "a Nantucket sleigh ride." Papa himself was laughing, and gradually my fear subsided. Surely he wouldn't look so happy if we were in any danger.

Thaddeus and I heaved sighs of relief as the whale turned again. It slowed as it grew tired, as did Papa's whaleboat. Now the line fell slack, and the men grabbed hold of it and began pulling themselves toward their quarry. As was customary, since it was always the officer's duty to kill the whale, Big John and Papa crouched down and exchanged places, Papa positioning himself at the clumsy cleat, lance in hand.

Closer, closer they drew until Papa was just a few feet away. As his boat pulled up alongside the great beast, he raised his lance, aimed, then jabbed it into its side. The crew pulled mightily on their oars as soon as he did this, for the whale began thrashing the water in its death throes.

It churned up the seas in an alarming fashion, setting Papa's boat to bobbing wildly, until finally a great spout of reddened foam burst from its blowhole.

"His chimney's afire!" shouted Thaddeus.

With one last writhe, the whale rolled fin out in the water and lay still. It was dead.

October 23, 1835

Thaddeus and I are confined to our quarters for the rest of the day. Sprigg was furious when he finally spotted us at the masthead, and hopped about on deck like an angry bee, stamping his feet and screeching threats at us in his raspy voice. We had to laugh at the sight, which didn't improve his temper. Only after he had promised not to tell Papa about our escapade would we agree to climb down.

We couldn't avoid his thimble, however, and my head still hurts from the thumping I received. And I am sorely disappointed not to see the whale towed in.

—P.

Seven

Now our whales are turned up and we're
prepared for our toil;
We will soon get on board with the blubber to boil.
When it's boiled out and stowed down in the hold,
We'll drink greasy luck to the whalers so bold.

—*The Cruise of the Dove*

No one warned me about the smell.

It was midafternoon by the time the dead whale
was towed back to the *Morning Star* and tied up
alongside. Though none of the other whaleboats had
succeeded in catching their prey, the men were
nonetheless exhausted from their efforts. They were
allowed only a brief rest and a quick meal before they
were back at it, however. They wouldn't stop now
until the cutting in was done. Sharks would make
quick work of a carcass left too long unattended.

Sprigg finally relented and allowed us back up on
deck, but only on the condition that we stay by his
side and keep out of the way of the men.

"The deck'll be slippery with gurry, and them sharp
spades can take off a man's hand or foot quicker than
Jack Flash," he said as we followed him up the companionway, and launched into a recital of gruesome

accidents he had personally witnessed over the years.

At the top, we paused for a moment, Thaddeus fairly dancing with impatience. Then a gust of breeze blew toward us.

"Ugh!" I cried, springing back in horror. "What is that vile smell?"

Sprigg lifted his nose into the air like a retriever and sniffed heartily.

"Smell?" he said. "Why that's the whale, of course! A sperm whale and a proper big 'un too, by the looks of it. And you a Nantucket girl—you mean to tell me you ain't smelled blood and blubber before?"

I shook my head. Of course we'd butchered chickens and an occasional pig on our little homestead, and the wharves could grow ripe in high summer, what with the fish and seaweed and rancid oil that sometimes leaked from the barrels stored on the docks and at the refinery, but if you put all of that together in one room on a hot day it wouldn't have smelled as appalling as this. Holding my handkerchief to my nose with one hand, I grabbed Thaddeus with the other and cautiously followed Sprigg to the siderail.

Taking care not to let go of the handkerchief, I propped my brother carefully on an overturned bucket and peered over the side of the *Morning Star*. The whale made an impressive sight. Its flukes were chained to the bow, and its long dark body stretched well past the waist of the ship, bobbing slightly in the gentle swell. The *Morning Star* listed heavily to starboard, anchored by the dead creature's massive weight. It seemed almost a pity to kill such a magnificent animal for our livelihood, but that was just the way of things, I supposed.

Papa was bawling orders to a handful of men as they opened the starboard gangway and swung a narrow scaffolding of planks out over the whale. Upon this precarious perch stood Cousin Jeremiah and second mate, Henry Chase, the latter sweating profusely.

"They'll be wise to mind their step on that cutting stage," cackled Sprigg. "Or they'll soon find themselves dinner for the sharks."

I spotted a pair of triangular fins slicing through the water below us, their owners hungry for the feast that would shortly come, and gripped Thaddeus a little tighter—it wouldn't do to have him go over the side today.

Once the cutting stage was lowered and secure, sharp spades were handed down to Cousin Jeremiah and Mr. Chase, who quickly began thrusting them into the carcass. With each gash, the water below them reddened.

"What did I tell you?" crowed Sprigg, pointing to the now busy sharks. "Look at those bloodthirsty beggars—worse than wolves, they are."

Shortly Cousin Jeremiah halted and waved to Mr. Macy, who gave a nod.

"Lower the blubber tackle!" the third mate ordered, trying to imitate Papa's Cape Horn bellow and looking sheepish when his voice broke on the final word.

A large iron hook suspended from a cluster of blocks swung out over the side and, after a little maneuvering, Cousin Jeremiah and Mr. Chase succeeded in jabbing it through the flap they had just cut in the whale's hide.

"Board ho!" Cousin Jeremiah called.

"Now, men!" ordered Papa, who was standing by the mainmast overseeing the proceedings. "Put your backs into it!"

The hands that were stationed at the windlass began to heave, the rope that led through the block and pulley to the giant hook grew taut, and the *Morning Star* listed even further starboard, until she was nearly standing on her beam ends. Slowly, very slowly, the whale began to turn in the water, just like a chicken on a spit. As it did, its dark skin and the thick yellowish blubber that was attached to it peeled back in one long strip.

"Just like an apple when you make pies, Patience!" cried Thaddeus.

Sprigg snorted. "Apple pie my foot," he scoffed.

"That's the blanket piece. Captain's son should know that."

Thaddeus looked crestfallen. I wanted to kick Sprigg, but restrained myself. We'd only be banished below again.

After the first long strip of blubber was aboard, more sharp instruments flashed in the sun as the crew began to cut it into greasy chunks. Others caught up the chunks with pitchforks or blubber gaffs and tossed them down through the main hatch, which had been opened to receive their offerings. Soon the deck was awash with blood and slime, and there was laughter as Long Tom and a German sailor named Schmidt slipped and fell in the slick mess. All of the men had rolled up their shirtsleeves and pant legs in a futile attempt to avoid getting dirty, and a number of them were barefoot. Spirits were high, and jokes and catcalls flew back and forth as they worked.

"What's down that hole, Sprigg?" I asked.

"The blubber room," he replied shortly. "Men'll be taking those horse pieces and cutting them into Bible leaves down there."

"Horse pieces? Bible leaves?"

"Watch and see."

Sure enough, after a short time the chunks of blubber emerged again, transformed. They had been sliced partway through into thinner pieces, just like the pages of a book.

"Why do they do that?" I asked, mystified.

Sprigg peered at me over his spectacles and heaved a sigh of disgust. "If you'd just clap a stopper to it and watch, you'd soon see," he said irritably. "Helps 'em try out quicker, is all."

This time I had to bite my lip to keep from answering back.

"Another sharp one, cooper!" cried Cousin Jeremiah. Behind us, Owen Gardiner was busy at his sharpening stone, grinding away at the spades and other cutting implements that quickly dulled in this monumental butchering.

Once the whale's forehead, or "junk," as they called it, was cut off and hoisted on deck, Papa had Big John climb right into the top of it. There he sloshed about with a bucket, ladling out a thick gray substance that was placed directly into barrels.

"He's baling the case for spermaceti," explained Sprigg, who, after his initial testiness, seemed to be warming to the role of tutor. "Finest oil known to man. Candles made from it are sold from here to London and Paris and back."

I had seen spermaceti candles at home, of course—they were produced in our island factory, and Mama always used them at our Sunday dinners—

but still, it was a bit of a shock to see where they actually came from.

Presently Sprigg—who, after all, had seen many a whale cut in—began to fidget.

"Time I got busy with evening chores," he said. "You children come down below with me now."

"But they won't be finished for ages!" Thaddeus protested. "Can't we stay up here?"

"Please, Sprigg. I promise we'll keep out of everyone's way," I added.

He regarded us suspiciously. "Oh very well," he snapped. "But don't you dare move an inch. I swear on my grandmother's thimble I'll give you the thumping of your lives if you get into trouble again."

We assured him we had no intention of doing so, and he stumped reluctantly off to the companionway, issuing a final warning as he went. "Stay well away from that tackle, and mind the decks, they'll soon be slippery!"

Sure enough, a short time later an oily, evil-smelling mixture began washing back toward where we were standing.

"Gurry," said Thaddeus with satisfaction.

"Ugh," I replied. "Come on, Tad."

And grabbing his hand again, I drew him toward the deckhouse, where we promptly broke our promise to Sprigg and climbed up onto our favorite perch atop the spare whaleboat.

Chips had a fire going beneath the twin try-pots, the enormous cauldrons in which the blubber sizzled and crackled as it was being rendered, and a puff of wind blew the greasy black smoke toward us.

Coughing, I pressed my handkerchief closer to my nose. "Maybe Sprigg was right, Tad," I said. "Let's go below."

"Just a bit longer!" he pleaded.

Curiosity got the better of me, and I relented.

Below us, the cooper was now busily cobbling together staves and iron hoops into the casks that would hold the oil. Chips continued to tend the flames, while on the tryworks platform Mr. Macy stirred the cauldron with a long ladle. Every so often he skimmed a few crisp scraps of blubber off the top and threw them into a spare pot that stood near him on deck.

"Just like when Martha cooks bacon," Thaddeus noted.

"I believe you're right about that," I replied.

"Chips says that once the blubber starts boiling, he won't need any more wood to keep the fire going," Thaddeus told me. "He just uses those clinkers."

"Those what?"

My brother nodded in the direction of the spare pot. "Clinkers. Those bacon—I mean blubber scraps."

"I declare, Tad, you are just a fountain of knowledge today," I told him. "You'll be a fine whaleman when you're older, just like Papa."

Thaddeus wriggled with pleasure at the praise, and I hoped it made up for Sprigg's sharp remarks earlier. It was hard for me to imagine Thaddeus ever being big enough to hunt whales, but that day would surely come, as it did for most Nantucket boys.

The light was fading now, and Papa ordered lanterns hung from the rigging. Their feeble glow helped illuminate the deck, as did the buglight—a metal basket filled with flaming clinkers that hung above the tryworks. It was an eerie scene, with the chimneys belching smoke and sparks and the flickering flames of the fire throwing monstrous shadows onto the ghostly sails above. With their soot-blackened faces and clothing all covered with grease and blood, the men looked like demons, and a sudden chill ran up my spine.

"Well, well, what have we 'ere, then?" said an unpleasantly familiar voice.

I whipped around to see two heads emerging above the midship shelter. It was Binyon and Todd! They must have taken advantage of nightfall to slip away for a moment.

"Couple of chickens ripe for the plucking, I'd say," said Binyon. A beefy arm shot out and grabbed

Thaddeus, who was too surprised to do anything but let out a startled squawk.

"I'd wager you thought we didn't remember you," said Todd, sniggering nastily, as the two of them dragged my brother to the deck. I scrambled down quickly after them.

"Let him go!" I cried.

"Not so fast, missy," said Binyon. His lips peeled back in a gap-toothed grin. "We've got some unfinished business with the lad."

Grabbing a rope, he whipped it around Thaddeus's waist and tied it tightly, glanced around quickly to make sure no one was looking, then heaved him over the far side of the *Morning Star*. I started to scream, but Todd clamped an oily hand over my mouth, stifling me.

"We 'eard he went overboard on his first day out, the poor mite, and so we took a notion to teach 'im how to swim," said Binyon with another humorless grin. He dragged the rope to and fro, and I could see Thaddeus dangling from it like a fish, gagging and choking as his tormentor dunked him into the dark water.

Twisting free, I launched myself at Binyon, pummeling his broad back with my fists. "Pull him up this instant you beast!"

The sailor turned and thrust his face close to

mine. His skin was as wind-weathered as old leather and his breath smelled worse than the gurry that sloshed about our ankles.

"Rope's a bit slippery," he said, flashing another repellent grin. "You startle me like that and I might lose my grip."

I thought of the sharks circling hungrily on the other side of the *Morning Star* and paled. "He's only *six*," I whispered furiously.

Binyon turned back to his task. "Shut 'er up, will you, Todd," he ordered.

His companion gripped me again, tighter this time. "It's all in fun, missy," he said, but I detected a note of worry in his voice. "He don't mean to hurt the lad."

In the dark water below, I could hear Thaddeus coughing and gasping for air. Frantically I twisted and turned, but Todd's hold on me only tightened. I had never felt so helpless in my life.

Suddenly a dark figure loomed behind us. It was Chips.

"Bring the boy up," he said quietly. In his hand he held a cutting spade.

"And if I don't?" blustered Binyon.

Beside me, Todd shifted nervously. Chips took a step forward, gripping the razor-sharp spade more tightly. "Delay any longer and you'll find out."

With a sneer, Binyon turned and hauled on the rope. Thaddeus came over the side and flopped limply onto the deck, soaked and shivering.

"Now release the girl," said Chips.

Todd let go of my arms and scuttled off into the darkness. I rushed over to my brother.

"Tad, it's all right, you're safe," I told him. I glared up at Binyon. "My Papa shall hear about this."

Some of the swagger went out of him at this. "It was only a jest, miss, honest," he whined. "Todd and me, we didn't mean no harm."

"Jest?" growled Chips. "Looked like the only one having any fun was you."

"Oh please, miss, don't tell the old man, he'll give us the cat for sure," pleaded Binyon.

I looked at him sharply, doubting his penitence. Every sailor feared the cat-o'-nine-tails. Still, flogging was a horrible sentence.

"Is it true, Chips? Will Papa whip these men for what they've done?"

"Most likely." The carpenter's face was impassive, and he hadn't relaxed his grip on the cutting spade.

I hesitated, torn between a desire to see Binyon and Todd punished and reluctance to cause anyone such pain.

"I'm begging you, miss," said Binyon. His eyes were downcast and there was a wheedling note in his voice. He certainly looked sorry enough.

"Oh, very well," I said crossly. "I shall say nothing."

Chips jerked the spade purposefully. "Away with you then, and don't let me catch you near these children again."

"Never in life," promised Binyon, trotting off with one last backward glance at me. I caught a gleam of something in his eyes—triumph, perhaps? or spite?—but it must only have been the reflection of the try-pot's flames.

October 25, 1835

Thaddeus is finally asleep. I managed to smuggle him past Glum and Sprigg, who were intent on a hand of whist, and got him out of his wet things and into bed. Glum had saved us some supper, but I told him (and it was true enough) that the gurry and the smell had nauseated us. Sprigg smirked at this news, the rat.

Though Tad seems to have overcome his fright, I remain deeply shaken, and not at all sure of the wisdom of not telling Papa what transpired tonight.

"Those two are nothing but trouble, Miss Patience," Chips said, when I thanked him for rescuing my brother yet again. Even Sprigg distrusts them, that I know. Since the day they boarded, they put the word out that they're old

shipmates keen for a taste of life aboard a blubber hunter, but Sprigg suspects otherwise.

"Old shipmates, is it?" I heard him observe to Glum. "Ha! Jumped shipmates is more likely. Those two have the smell of the British navy on them, and I'd wager my grandmother's thimble they're deserters both."

Whatever the truth of their former life, with their quarrelsome ways and rough tongues, Bunion and Toad are to be given a wide berth. Whether I should tell Papa of our encounter tonight is another matter, but I have given my word. Oh, how I wish that Mama or Aunt Anne were here, as they would surely know what to do!

Work on our first whale—my whale—will be finished by dawn, Sprigg says, and what remains of the carcass cut loose, to the further delight of the sharks. The whale's enormous teeth will be carefully pulled out and given to the crew, who prize them for their scrimshandering.

Papa will be pleased with our take—Glum estimates at least fifty barrels of oil, a very respectable haul for a sperm whale. And now that our ship has been properly greased, her luck should be even better, they tell me.

I must confess I had no idea that whale hunting was such a dirty, smelly business. But Sprigg

and Glum assure me that once the Morning Star
has been scoured and scrubbed from stem to stern,
she will look like a proper ship again, instead of
some wretched butcher's shop. Everything will
gleam but the sails, now dulled from the smoke of
the tryworks. At last I understand why whalers
return home looking so down-at-heels. By the
time we sail back into Nantucket harbor, our sails
will be the same dingy brown as all the rest.

—P.

Eight

Two things break the monotony
Of an Atlantic trip:
Sometimes alas you ship a sea,
Sometimes you see a ship.

—*Most Beautiful*

Two days of squalls and dense fog followed the excitement of our first whale hunt, with rain and sea and sky alike as gray as a gull feather. Thaddeus and I spent most of our time below, listening to the gusts rattling the window in Papa's day cabin and bored to the brink of tears, though just as glad for the chance to steer clear of Binyon and Todd. Finally, on the third morning, the sun reappeared and Sprigg allowed us back up on deck after breakfast.

There we discovered that the pigs had been brought up from the hold for an airing. Thaddeus was enchanted by this sight, and after feeding the chickens and milking Daisy he went into the makeshift pen to visit them, but forgot to latch it on his way out.

Quicker than Jack Flash, as Sprigg would say, piglets exploded across the foredeck like popcorn in a hot skillet.

"Whoa there!" shouted Mr. Chase. "Belay those pigs!"

Thaddeus let out a yelp as the angry mother pig lunged for his heels. In his haste to evade her sharp teeth, he collided with Mr. Chase and sent him sprawling. Several of the hands rushed to help Mr. Chase, and soon sails were flapping, lines were all atangle, and Mr. Chase and Cousin Jeremiah and Mr. Macy were all three bawling orders at the men, their voices barely audible above the squealing of the pigs.

The racket brought Papa up from his day cabin. Unfortunately for me, he arrived just as I was informing Thaddeus in no uncertain terms that he was an infernal scrub.

"Thunder and lightning, Patience!" Papa roared. "That is hardly language befitting a young lady! And certainly not a Goodspeed!"

My mouth dropped open. I had heard far worse from his own lips these past weeks. Papa pointed toward the companionway, a pious expression on his face, and said, "Below. You are confined to your quarters until further notice."

"But Papa—" I protested.

My father's eyebrows flew together in that ferocious scowl which always meant foul weather ahead. "I'll stand for no mutiny aboard my ship!" he warned.

Burning with the injustice of it—I wasn't the one who caused the ruckus, after all—I stalked off.

"And you men there do something about those infernal pigs!" Papa shouted behind me.

It was stuffy in our stateroom, and I opened the window in Papa's day cabin to let in some air. I busied myself for a bit tidying up what little mess there was—Thaddeus's things, of course, I noted resentfully—remade the beds, and put the clothes that lay on Papa's bunk away, then sat down on my own bunk and reached for my journal.

October 28, 1835

Things I miss at sea:
1. *The smell of cool, damp earth.*
2. *Flowers.*
3. *My cat, Patches.*
4. *The color green—green leaves, green grass, green anything. Seaweed doesn't count.*
5. *The company of women (unexpected).*
6. *Fresh butter for my bread.*
7. *Mama, who would never have sent me below for using the word "infernal."*

—P.

The distant clatter of pots in the galley did nothing to improve my humor. Even slaving away under Glum's sharp eye would have been better than this unjust imprisonment. Glum resented my presence in the galley as much as I resented being there, and there was always much rattling of utensils and muttering about the foolishness of bringing children aboard whaling ships whenever I appeared, but he had accustomed himself to my presence, and we had existed in a state of armed truce ever since he discovered that I knew my way around a kitchen.

By now the crew fairly doted on my biscuits, and I was much petted and praised for my pies. Glum suffered the implied insult to his own abilities in his usual doleful silence. If the truth were told, he wasn't much of a cook, though the crew seemed satisfied with their monotonous daily rations—great vats of pickled beef they called "salt horse," mushy dried peas, and hardtack, which were nasty, tasteless, flinty ship's biscuits crawling with weevils. For a treat, they were given duff on Sundays, a revolting pudding made with flour, lard, raisins, and apples, and served topped with molasses.

Those of us at the captain's table fared slightly better. Though Glum's culinary efforts for us weren't fancy, he made a credible chowder and succeeded well enough with other plain dishes.

Suddenly from above I heard a cry of "Sail ho!"

Racing to the window in the day cabin, I peered through the Tad-Catcher. Sure enough, another ship was approaching us.

There was a tap on the cabin door.

"Yes?" I said.

The door opened a crack. It was Thaddeus. He eyed me silently for a moment. "I'm sorry about the pigs," he said finally.

It was hard to stay angry with my little brother for long. "Never mind about the pigs now, Tad. I shouldn't have called you a scrub."

"An infernal scrub," he said with some relish.

I smiled. "Yes."

"Papa says you may come up on deck again."

I wasted no time in following my brother back up the companionway. This was the first ship we had seen in our weeks at sea, after all, and I didn't want to miss it.

She turned out to be a fellow Nantucket whaler, the *Rambler*, whose captain was an old acquaintance of Papa's. Eager for news, both ships quickly hove to, and once the yards were taken aback and the sails shortened and trimmed, we rocked gently side by side.

"You're a sight for sore eyes, Captain Russell!" Papa hollered through his speaking trumpet.

"As are thee, Isaiah Goodspeed," Captain Russell boomed back. "Where are thee bound for?"

"Fayal," said Papa.

"Our destination as well."

"Is that Mrs. Russell I spy?"

"It is indeed."

Captain Russell's wife, a sturdy-looking woman with rosy cheeks, smiled broadly and fluttered her handkerchief at us. Thaddeus and I, who were standing by Papa on our usual perches—a pair of overturned buckets—waved back. It was clear from Mrs. Russell's plain, dove gray cloak and bonnet, Captain Russell's broad-brimmed black hat, and their singular manner of speech that they were both Quakers, as were many of our Nantucket friends and neighbors.

"How many barrels?" Papa asked.

"Nary a one," Captain Russell replied. "And thee?"

"Sixty. We took a sperm bull a week ago."

"Capital! No doubt thee owes thy greasy luck to thy children. Young ones bring good fortune aboard a whaler, thee knows."

Papa spared us a quizzical glance. "So I've been told."

"Perhaps thee will lend them to me for a spell," continued Captain Russell. "That fine fellow at thy side looks like a proper sailor, with every finger a fishhook."

Hearing this, Thaddeus inched closer to me, and Papa laughed.

"Pray come aboard for dinner, and bring thy good luck charms as well. Mrs. Russell and I would welcome thy company."

And thus began our first gam, what whalemen call a visit at sea. Papa had his whaleboat lowered, and Thaddeus and I were handed down by Chips to Big John. The decks of both ships were abuzz with activity as the men prepared for their own gam. As was tradition, the captains and their boat crews would visit on one ship, while the mates and their crews gammed on the other. Binyon and Todd, I was happy to note, would be remaining behind aboard the *Morning Star*.

The day was sunny and fine, and spirits were high at this welcome break in routine. Once alongside the *Rambler,* Papa clambered nimbly aboard, but Mrs. Russell insisted that Thaddeus and I use her gamming chair, an odd but practical contraption made from a barrel that had been partially cut away, hung with ropes, and fitted inside with a plank for a seat. Two of the *Rambler*'s hands hooked it to a pulley at one of the davits above us and lowered it to our whaleboat. Big John steadied it as Thaddeus and I climbed in, and we were soon hoisted aboard in grand style.

A quick tour of the ship was followed by dinner below. Mrs. Russell proved a lively hostess, and over the meal regaled us with a steady stream of amusing tales about the *Rambler*'s crew.

"As verdant a crop of greenies as ever I've seen," agreed Captain Russell, shaking his head. "Like the moors out Madaket way in springtime."

His wife was a woman who heartily enjoyed her own wit, and by the time she got to telling us about a poor fellow who was in the habit of stuffing a red neckerchief in his mouth whenever he got into a whaleboat, she was laughing so hard she could barely squeeze the words out.

"Does he do this for luck?" asked Papa, as mystified as Thaddeus and I.

"No, and that's the wonder of it!" Mrs. Russell replied, gasping for breath. "He can't swim, and somewhere he got the notion that if he stoppered himself up with a wad of cloth it would keep him afloat were he to fall overboard! Just like a cork in a bottle!"

A whoop of laughter went up at this, and Papa added to the hilarity with an account of the day Charlie Fishback was strung up from the main yard by his ankle.

After dinner we ventured back on deck. The men were lounging in the sunshine on the foredeck, smoking their pipes and scratching away at bits of scrimshaw. Long Tom had brought along his fiddle, and he embarked on a merry tune that Thaddeus and I knew well by now. When they reached the chorus we joined in, linking arms and spinning about as we sang: "So be cheery, my lads! Let your hearts never fail, while the bold harpooneer is astriking of the whale!"

A cheer went up from the assembled crowd when we finished, and Captain Russell pronounced us "saltier than Lot's wife," while his wife pretended to inspect Thaddeus's pockets for a bilge-pump, much to the amusement of the crew.

Captain Russell then took Papa down into the hold, Thaddeus took off after the cabin boy in search of the ship's cat, who was rumored to have kittens stashed somewhere aboard, and I accompanied Mrs. Russell below for tea.

The *Rambler*'s day cabin was a cheerful place, with pots of geraniums lining the stern windows, a framed print of Daniel in the lion's den on the wall, and even a turkey carpet painted on the floor. As we settled in, Mrs. Russell plied me with questions about relatives and neighbors whom she knew on Nantucket. Normally, I would have found this kind of exchange as dull as an old penny, but Mrs. Russell had such a keen sense of humor and expressed such an affectionate interest in me, that I found her company immensely cheering.

Soon, there came the sound of feet on the companionway stairs and Thaddeus popped in, lugging an enormous gray cat.

"Patience!" he cried. "This is Abigail. She has five kittens and we searched and searched for them and finally found them in the hold in a box of cloth—"

"Not my quilt pieces!" cried Mrs. Russell in alarm.

"But we couldn't bring them because she got angry and scratched us, so I just brought her so you could see her because I know you miss Patches." With that, he dumped her unceremoniously on my lap. "Can I have some cake, please?"

"May I," I said automatically.

Mrs. Russell gave him a generous slice, and he fell on it like a starving man.

"I wish we had a ship's cat," mumbled Thaddeus, his mouth full of cake.

"Does thee now," said Mrs. Russell, with a speculative glance at Abigail. "Well, I know a tabby who will need a new home if I find she's been nesting in my quilt pieces."

After the last bit of cake had been eaten and the teapot drained of its final drop, our gam drew to a close. We parted company reluctantly, with mutual promises to meet ashore in Fayal.

October 29, 1835

Papa reviewed our schoolwork for the first time tonight. Thaddeus read aloud to him from the Bible, the story of Noah and the ark, and when he finished Papa patted his head and said he was doing very well indeed.

Then it was my turn. I showed him some of the mathematical equations I have been working and his eyebrows shot up.

"Jeremiah, look at this," he said.

Cousin Jeremiah winked at me. "I've been telling you all along, Isaiah," he said.

"As did Caroline," Papa replied, giving me a thoughtful look. "This is fine work, my girl, fine work indeed. I have been most remiss in letting my responsibility for the Morning Star overshadow my fatherly duties."

Something that had been clenched tight inside me unfurled at his words like a sail in a fresh breeze. A smile slowly spread across my face, drawing an answering smile from Papa.

"Well," he said briskly, after a moment. "We shall just have to see about this. For now, it's time you and your brother were in bed."

He didn't say any more after that, but oh, how my heart is gladdened to know that he is pleased with me!

—P.

Nine

Trust not too much your opinion
When your vessel's under way.
Let good advice bear dominion,
A compass will not stray.

—*Most Beautiful*

Later that night I awoke to find Papa standing by my bunk, shaking me gently by the shoulder.

"Shhhh," he whispered. "Don't wake your brother. Get your cloak and come up on deck."

Sleepy and confused—and vastly puzzled by this turn of events—I did as he bid me and emerged a short time later to find him waiting for me by the deckhouse. Schmidt was standing his trick at the helm, and he lifted a forefinger to his cap as I shuffled past him, yawning.

"So," said Papa gruffly. "You want to learn to navigate."

Suddenly I was wide awake. "Oh yes, please!" I said, nodding my head vigorously.

"This is all Jeremiah's idea," he continued. "But perhaps there's sense to what he says. You've a mind for mathematics, my girl, there's no denying that."

I didn't quite know what to make of this praise, and stared at my feet.

"You won't learn about the stars by examining the deck," said Papa. "Up with your chin, now, and let's get started."

I obeyed, and gazing around me discovered that it was a glorious night. Only the faintest of breezes rustled in the canvas above, and the moon lay off the starboard quarter, as fat and round as a Dutch cheese. The water's tranquil surface shimmered with dappled silver light, as if all the stars had fallen from the heavens, their cold fire still burning bright beneath the surface of the sea.

"It's beautiful," I breathed.

Papa grunted. "Night sailing can be pleasant," he agreed. Taking me by the arm, he steered me forward until we were just beneath the mainmast.

Papa was silent for a long while. Much to my surprise, when he finally began to speak, it was not about the sky, however.

"You said once that I shouldn't have gone away, that had I remained on Nantucket your mother might not have fallen ill." He hesitated for a moment, then continued. "Believe me, my girl, not a day has passed since I returned to find her gone that I have not wondered the same thing myself. But I'm a whaleman by trade and cannot make my living ashore."

He paused again, his gaze fixed on the heavens. "Perhaps you think I didn't love your mother, Patience, but nothing could be further from the truth."

"Oh Papa, I'm so sorry I said those things!" I blurted. "Mama always chided me for letting my temper rule my tongue."

My father looked down and gave me a rueful smile. "It would appear to run in the family," he said. "I too have said things I regretted these past weeks. I know how keenly you desired to stay home, but you and your brother are all I have left of your mama now, and the thought of leaving you behind once again, well—"

It was more than I could bear. I flung myself at him and buried my head in his coat. Putting his arms around me, Papa kissed the top of my head and comforted me until the flood of tears subsided.

"Look," he said gently, handing me his handkerchief and directing my gaze off past the port waist boat to the Big Dipper. "You see that star there, the one that the far side of the ladle is pointing to?"

I nodded, sniffling.

"That's Polaris, the North Star."

"Your meeting star!" I exclaimed. Mama used to love to tell me of this star, which she and Papa had promised to gaze upon every night they were apart, to draw comfort from the knowledge that they were thinking of each other.

"I still think of your mother every time I see that star," said Papa.

"Perhaps she thinks of you, too," I replied shyly.

Papa squeezed my shoulder. "I'm sure she does.

In fact, I'm sure she thinks of all of us—you, me, and Tad."

"Shall it be our family meeting star from now on?" I suggested.

"That's a capital idea, Patience!"

And so my navigation lesson began with a star destined to hold a special place in my heart forever. Soon my head was swimming with the names of constellations and unfamiliar terms—declination, right ascension, latitude, longitude, and the like—but it was with a newly joyful spirit that I returned to my bunk an hour later.

The following morning I was awake at dawn. It was the first of November, my birthday! Moving quietly so as not to waken Thaddeus, I dressed and crept up on deck.

"Well if it isn't the birthday girl!" said Cousin Jeremiah.

He was standing at the helm with Papa and Charlie Fishback, the latter nervously gripping the wheel with white-knuckled hands.

"Morning, miss," Charlie said, letting go barely long enough to touch his cap in greeting. "Many happy returns."

"I do believe she's grown an inch taller since yesterday, Jeremiah," added Papa with a smile. "A very happy birthday to you, my girl!"

"Thank you, Papa," I said.

"Long Tom's just been up at the masthead, and he tells us that Pico is visible, so Fayal should be fetching up on the horizon anytime now. Hold her steady there, Fishback, while I take my daughter forward."

Puzzled, I followed him toward the bow.

"Not a word to your brother about this," he said, boosting me up onto the narrow platform that arced across the very front of our ship, just behind the bowsprit. "He'd be over the side quicker than Sprigg can say Jack Flash. Keep tight hold of the forestay."

I must have still looked perplexed, for he added, "It's the best place to see landfall."

The sun climbed steadily higher, and with its light and warmth came birds—petrels and gulls that wheeled overhead, their cries tossed toward us by the wind. In a short time the island of Fayal appeared on the horizon, a low, dark bump that grew steadily larger as we approached. Mr. Chase rang the bell behind me to announce the changing of the watch, and there were thumps and voices from below as the hands tumbled up from the fo'c'sle. They looked surprised to see me standing at the bow, but word quickly got around that it was my birthday, and by the time we approached the harbor nearly every member of the crew had managed to sidle up and wish me many happy returns of the day—with the notable exception of Binyon and Todd, who kept a wary distance.

Glum served doughnuts for breakfast, in my honor, and to his credit they were quite good, but despite our lavish praise he only shook his head and said dolefully, "I've made better." Afterward, we returned above deck, and Papa relented and allowed Thaddeus to join me forward, charging Sprigg to keep him out of harm's way.

For once, Sprigg didn't complain. The deck grew crowded as we drew closer to land, as everyone strained for the first glimpse of the harbor, but ours was the best vantage point. The sun was high overhead now, hot on my shoulders, and Thaddeus wriggled with excitement beside me.

"Will you not keep still," Sprigg said crossly. "Bouncing about won't get us there any faster."

Thaddeus ignored him. "Look, Patience!" he cried. "Trees!"

"Well of course there are trees, you lumpkin," chided Sprigg. "What did you expect?"

Even Sprigg's annoyance couldn't dampen Thaddeus's spirits, however, and he continued to skip up and down with delight as Papa gave orders to shorten sail. The harbor was a forest of masts. We quickly spied a number of fellow Nantucket whalers—the *Franklin,* the *Orion,* and the *Sarah Ann*—and dropped anchor by the *Rambler*. Captain and Mrs. Russell had already gone ashore, but Papa gave their steward instructions to extend an invitation to my birthday dinner.

"We'll be at the Hotel Fayal," he called. "Seven o'clock sharp!"

Both watches slipped below to change into shore-going clothes, trading stained and tattered workaday garments for duck trousers, smart blue jackets, and the round black hats that distinguished those in the whaling trade. I spotted Charlie Fishback next to Big John, both looking very fine and clearly eager for a day ashore.

After Papa dismissed the crew, admonishing them to keep their wits about them and steer clear of pickpockets, he turned to us.

"I'll take the children off your hands for the day, Sprigg," he said. "Chips and Glum have volunteered to act as shipkeepers while we lay on fresh supplies, so you're free to go ashore yourself."

Sprigg's wrinkled old face split into a broad grin, and he lost no time in clambering down into a waiting boat.

"Mr. Folger, see if you can rustle up a few more able seamen to complete our crew," said Papa to Cousin Jeremiah. "There should be plenty of men ashore eager to sign onto a ship as trim as the *Morning Star*."

"Aye, sir," said Cousin Jeremiah, who sketched a wave to Thaddeus and me as he, too, disappeared over the side.

Satisfied that everything aboard the *Morning Star* was shipshape and Bristol fashion, and that there was no chance she would float off in his absence, Papa finally called for his whaleboat and handed Thaddeus and me down to Big John.

As we pulled for shore, I looked around me. I had never seen any harbor other than our own, and Fayal's was lovely. Crescent-shaped, it was crowded with tidy whitewashed houses whose rust-colored roofs rose up along the gentle slopes to the hills beyond.

Once ashore Thaddeus and I found to our chagrin that while we had gained our sea legs these past weeks, we had most definitely lost our land legs. Papa roared with laughter as we staggered across the dock and onto the street.

"I can see I shall have to hire a carriage for the day," he said, wiping the tears from his eyes. "Can't have you two lurching about like a pair of tipsy sailors now, can I?"

We toured the island until dinnertime, and although I was sorely tempted to spend my silver dollar, it stayed in my pinafore pocket. It had become a sort of good luck charm, and I was reluctant to part with it. At the hotel Papa took rooms for us, and a maid whisked me off to a hot bath, then buttoned me into a clean dress and adorned my hair with a blossom plucked from the vase on my dressing table, all the while rattling away in Portuguese.

Promptly at seven, Papa knocked at my door, and we went down to the lobby, where Cousin Jeremiah, Captain and Mrs. Russell, and the mates from the two ships awaited us.

"Doesn't thee look cunning with that flower in thy hair," said Mrs. Russell, patting my cheek.

Dinner was a veritable feast, crowned with a heavenly lemon sherbet that Papa had ordered especially for my birthday.

"A toast to the guest of honor," said Captain Russell as the last bite was finished, rising and raising his glass. "To Patience, on the occasion of her thirteenth birthday. May she have fresh winds and fair skies on the voyage ahead, and may she bring the *Morning Star* greasy luck!"

A cry of "Hear, hear!" was taken up around the table, and my face turned pink with embarrassment and pleasure.

Then came the presents—a potted geranium and some hair ribbons from Captain and Mrs. Russell, a book of poems by William Wordsworth and a basket of pretty seashells from Cousin Jeremiah, a bag of oranges from Mr. Chase and Mr. Macy, and from Thaddeus, a long, thin piece of whalebone on which he had scratched my name and a crude likeness of the *Morning Star.*

"Chips helped me," he said, beaming proudly. "You can use it to mark the place in your books."

Papa astonished me with not one but two presents—a dear little gray kitten (courtesy of Abigail, who had indeed made a nest in Mrs. Russell's quilt pieces) and, as if that wasn't treasure enough, a blue velvet box that opened to reveal a strand of pearls.

A collective sigh went around the table as I held them up, their subtle, shimmering beauty reflected in the candlelight.

"Oh, Papa," I breathed, for I knew these pearls very well. Had I not seen them on a thousand Sundays, clasped around the throat of the one I loved best in all the world? "These were your wedding gift to Mama."

"Yes, and who better to wear them than our lovely daughter?" he replied.

I bit my lip in a vain attempt to hold back tears, and bent over the necklace to busy myself with its clasp. Mrs. Russell helped me fasten it, and the pearls encircled my neck like a warm embrace. Mama suddenly felt very near.

"Thank you, Papa," I whispered, and it seemed to me that my father's eyes were as moist as my own.

Papa cleared his throat and thrust yet another parcel into my hands.

"This is from your Aunt Anne," he said. "She gave me strict instructions not to give it to you until today."

Wrapped in plain brown paper and tied up with string, the square package was surprisingly heavy. Inside was a handsome polished wood box with a brass plate affixed to the cover, upon which were engraved my initials: PCG. My middle name was Caroline, after Mama. I opened the box and gasped—it was a sextant!

Smaller than Papa's, it fitted neatly in my hand, and its brass casing felt cool and smooth to the touch. There was a note as well. I cleared my throat and read it aloud: "Dearest Patience, Miss Mitchell joins me in wishing you the happiest of birthdays. We picked this out for you at Mr. Tilton's chandlery. Always remember that your mother expected great things of you, and so do we. Your loving Aunt Anne."

Papa stared at the sextant for a long moment, then burst out laughing.

"Trust Anne to have long since determined which way the wind was blowing!" he said, shaking his head.

"Planning to make a navigator out of her, are thee,

Isaiah?" asked Captain Russell curiously.

"Apparently my sister thinks so," replied Papa, still chuckling. "It cannot be denied, however, that my daughter has an aptitude for arithmetic."

Back aboard the *Morning Star* the next day there were more surprises. Charlie Fishback, cap in hand, approached me as I boarded, smiling shyly.

"I made this for you," he said, passing me a piece of line that displayed a series of slightly grubby knots. They were lumpy and uneven and reminded me of one of my samplers.

"I'm not very good at tying knots yet," he admitted, "but I thought you might use it to string through your silver dollar for a necklace."

"That's a splendid idea, Charlie!" I replied in delight. "What a lovely present."

Then, as I passed the galley, Glum stepped out and thrust a package into my hands, scowling. I opened it to find a whalebone jagging wheel, just like the one Martha used in our kitchen at home for crimping the edges of piecrusts. Its handle was skillfully and elaborately carved into the shape of a porpoise.

"You make good biscuits, but the gunwales on your pies want gussying up," he muttered, with his usual lack of enthusiasm.

I glowed. This was high praise indeed, coming from Glum.

"Why, Glum, this is beautiful!" I said. "Thank you very much."

I looked up. There was something oddly unfamiliar about his appearance, and it took me a moment to realize that he was smiling.

Ten

"Oh pilot, 'tis a fearful night;
There's danger on the deep.
I'll come and pace the deck with thee;
I do not dare to sleep."
"Go down, go down," the pilot cries,
"This is no place for thee;
Fear not but trust in Providence
Wherever thou mayst be."

—*The Pilot*

November 15, 1835

No wind, no whales now for nearly a week.

We left Fayal with a hold full of water and fresh stores and picked up the tradewinds directly. A solid fortnight of fine sailing followed as we were pushed toward South America by a smacking breeze, and we even managed to take another sperm whale, along with three blackfish, which is well, as they fuel the lamps aboard the Morning Star *and our supply had grown low. Papa says we have nearly a hundred barrels of prime oil already, a fine start to our voyage.*

Now, however, we are becalmed in the dol-

drums, lolling on that windless stretch of sea that lies between the northeast and southeast trades and bedevils sailing ships. Papa has declared make-and-mend to keep the hands from mischief and all of us from going mad. The Morning Star fairly gleams from all the swabbing and polishing and painting she has received these past few days, while Thaddeus and I have tidied and retidied our tiny stateroom a dozen times. Cousin Jeremiah fusses with the logbook like a medieval monk with a manuscript, adding flourishes and embellishments and small drawings to the margins, and even Glum has been busy, turning out the galley and scrubbing it from top to bottom. This morning he pressed Sprigg into service, and as I write this the two of them are seated on overturned buckets, taking inventory of the provisions, both of them as irritable as owls.

There is one benefit to the enforced idleness, however, as Thaddeus and I have received a windfall of small gifts from the crew—whalebone whistles and egg cups, napkin rings for each of us, miniature animals for Thaddeus, and even a doll bed for Miranda, courtesy of Chips.

Still, it's exceedingly dull, as well as hot, the closer we draw to the equator. Papa says there's nothing to be done about the lack of wind but wait. "What can't be cured must be endured," he says. But sailors are a superstitious lot, and I often see them furtively whistling in a vain attempt to call up a breeze.

So far the only thing that answers is my new kitten, whose ears perk up at the sound. He's a dear little thing, gray like his mother, but with a comical white tip to his tail that gives it the look of a paintbrush. I have named him Ishmael. He's curled up asleep right now on the deckhouse sofa beside me. Perhaps I'll curl up for a nap too. It's not as if there's anything else to do.

—P.

The southern tradewinds finally picked up and ferried us to Rio, a lively port that's a favorite amongst the hands, by the sound of the hearty cheers that went up when it hove into view. We spent an agreeable few days exploring the city, and Papa again booked us into a hotel, a very grand one this time. We even took in a band concert. Before we knew it, however, we were all back aboard the *Morning Star* and under way again.

"There'll be plenty of time for dillydallying later, once we're round the Horn," Papa said. "This is the best time of year to make the passage, and I'll rest easier once Tierra del Fuego is well behind us."

It grew colder with each passing day, and the seas

grew rougher as well. The winds picked up, and at times our ship was tossed about like a leaf. Papa grew snappish and kept to himself, spending long hours pacing the deck. Our navigation lessons ceased.

"His face is as long as a Fayal goat's," grumbled Sprigg, who had ventured to interrupt Papa's pacing with a simple question and had nearly had his ears boxed in return.

On one day when we were suffering a particularly ugly cross-sea—even Daisy was seasick—I asked Cousin Jeremiah if this was what it was like at Cape Horn. His lips twisted into a wry smile.

"We've not even reached the Roaring Forties yet," was all he said in reply.

I broke out our winter clothing from the sea chests, and Thaddeus and I wrapped ourselves in flannel and wool from head to toe. We rarely ventured up on deck now, though mercifully the galley stayed warm enough, as Glum and I brewed up an endless parade of stews, chowders, and pots of hot coffee to help keep us all from freezing to death. Belowdecks Sprigg kept the potbellied stove in the main cabin burning briskly, and with the door to Papa's day cabin propped open, it stayed cozy enough during the day. At night he slipped heated bricks wrapped in flannel into our beds to keep our feet toasty.

Ishmael could usually be found curled into a tight ball at the base of the stove, napping. He was growing into a handsome cat, and showed every sign of becoming a prodigious mouser. Though he hadn't yet tackled the bilge rats, who were notoriously fierce, the remains of many a mouse were left proudly displayed at the foot of my bunk. He had also become a favorite with the crew, who spoiled him shamelessly.

Since our encounter on the night of the first cutting-in, Binyon and Todd had turned their attention from Thaddeus and me to Charlie Fishback, whom they bullied ceaselessly, needling him about his red hair, calling him "Firetop" and "Charlie Horseback" and plaguing him about his clumsiness, which was hardly fair, as he was not nearly as green now as when we first left Nantucket and could reef and steer handily.

Though I had kept my word and not informed Papa of our run-in, I found it impossible to hold my tongue in the face of their cruelty to Charlie, and pressed Papa to put them ashore at the Falkland Islands. Even when I told him that they taunted me as well, calling me "bluestocking" and "Mistress Put-on-Airs" when they spied me taking readings with my sextant or puzzling over the altitude correction tables in Bowditch's *New American Practical Navigator*, Papa refused to listen. He just said I mustn't interfere, that it was the way of things at sea, and that it would all sort itself out before long.

"They'll grow tired of the sport soon enough," he said. "Besides, both of them are able hands, and with Cape Horn ahead of us, the *Morning Star* needs every man she has got."

What the *Morning Star* really needed, I was sorely tempted to say, was a good woman aboard. Mama, for instance. She despised insolence as much as she did sulking—"you could ride that lip to 'Sconset," she would tell me at the slightest sign of a pout—and she would certainly have had Binyon and Todd off the ship quicker than Jack Flash. Papa was deaf to my pleas, however.

One morning in late December, we finally reached the latitude of the Cape. Papa ordered our course changed to westward, and I persuaded Glum to let me make taffy for the crew as a Christmas treat.

"You'll need to fetch a keg of molasses from the hold," he said reluctantly. "Get the key to the store-room from your father, and take one of the crew with you to carry it up."

I glanced around to see who might be willing to help me, and caught a flash of red hair in the rigging. Charlie Fishback was climbing back down toward the deck.

"Mr. Macy, might I borrow Charlie for a minute?" I asked the third mate, explaining my task.

"Why certainly, Miss Patience. You may even have him for two," he replied with a smile, inclining his head.

It was dark as a stack of black cats in the hold, and chilly. Charlie lit the whale oil lantern that I had brought with me and held it up. We could see our breath.

"This way," I said, taking the lantern from him and picking my way carefully amongst the casks and boxes. "Mind your head."

There was a scrabbling noise nearby and I jumped.

"What was that?" I cried.

"Rats, most likely. Not to worry, Miss Patience, they'll keep their distance."

I shuddered and drew my skirt in close around me, but we reached the storeroom door without incident. As I unlocked it I asked, "Are you still homesick, Charlie?"

He cleared his throat behind me in embarrassment. "I'm growing accustomed to being at sea."

"And Bunion and Toad, are they still making sport of you?"

"Who?" he asked, mystified.

"Oh, that's what Tad and I call Binyon and Todd," I explained.

He burst out laughing. "It suits them, miss, it

truly does! I must remember that. Oh, I suppose they still gally me now and then, but I do my best to pay them no mind. Last time Big John caught them at it, he gave them a taste of his knuckles."

"I'm very glad to hear it," I said. "It's about time your shipmates showed some gumption and knocked those two down a peg."

We found the molasses without any trouble, but as Charlie bent to heave it onto his shoulder, my gaze fell on a long, coffin-shaped box nearby. I drew in my breath sharply.

"What?" Charlie asked in alarm.

I pointed wordlessly at the box on the floor, and he set the keg of molasses back down.

"Is it, is it—" I began.

"No, Miss Patience. It couldn't be."

Together we pried the lid off gingerly. The flickering light from my lamp caught a gleam of metal inside.

"Why look!" I cried. "There are pistols, and rifles—even a sword! Whatever is Papa doing with weapons aboard the *Morning Star*?"

We stared at the contents of the box in wonderment.

"I've heard tell in the fo'c'sle of South Sea islands where the natives are none too friendly," said Charlie. "Kanaka Jim showed me a spear tipped with shark's teeth he says he got in Nuku Hiva. And you remember what happened aboard the *Globe*."

Indeed I did. Like the *Essex,* the tragedy aboard the *Globe* had taken place years ago, but the tale was equally familiar to any child growing up on Nantucket. A foremast hand had incited the crew to mutiny, and took the ship after murdering poor Captain Worth and the three mates.

"How did you hear of it?" I asked.

"Long Tom told us of it one evening during the dogwatch," Charlie replied. He replaced the lid on the box. "Captain's got good reason to carry arms."

Unsettled by our discovery, I relocked the storeroom and we retraced our steps through the hold in silence, climbed up the ladder into steerage, then up another ladder onto the main deck where we walked right into Binyon and Todd.

"Sweet on the captain's daughter are ye, farmboy?" jeered Binyon.

I turned on him furiously. "Clap a stopper to it, Bunion, and leave poor Charlie be!"

Binyon's eyes narrowed. "You've a sharp tongue, missy."

Fortunately Mr. Macy chose that moment to round the mainmast.

"Is there some difficulty here, Miss Patience?" he asked.

I glared at Binyon, knowing that it would only go worse for Charlie if I tattled to the watch officer.

"None whatsoever, Mr. Macy," I replied.

"*Bunion*—I mean Binyon here was just lending us a hand with the molasses."

I felt a rush of spiteful pleasure as Binyon reddened, and a smile crept across Mr. Macy's face.

"Ah yes," he said. "Well, then, ah, Binyon, if you're finished, you and Todd there can nip aloft and clap a hand onto the main yard. Captain says we're in for a blow."

The captain was right. All day the barometer continued to drop as Glum and I struggled with the taffy, which was no easy task on a windless afternoon in my own kitchen at home, let alone in a tiny galley on a ship lurching mightily with each roll of the sea. Still, we managed it.

By late afternoon the sea was running strong and the wind blowing so hard that it took two men to hold one man's hair on, as Papa liked to say. Glum made an early supper—pancakes—but Thaddeus and I were the only ones able to enjoy them, as Papa had called all hands on deck. While we gamely chased our plates around the heaving table, we could hear Papa and the mates hollering at the crew.

"Aloft there, and shorten sail before we're blown to Halifax!"

"Bear a hand now!"

"Steady at the wheel, man, hold her to her course!"

Afterward, while Sprigg staggered about clearing

our supper dishes away, his gray pigtail bobbing wildly as he reeled toward the pantry—from which emerged shortly the sound of smashing crockery, followed by a string of curses—Thaddeus and I grabbed our wraps and crept up the companionway to see for ourselves what all the fuss was about.

It was sheeting rain, and icy water sluiced toward us across the deck of the *Morning Star* as she pitched and rolled in the heavy seas. The wind shook the shrouds above us and sent a mix of rain and seawater stinging across my face. Brushing my hair aside I peered forward.

"Thunder and lightning!" I gasped. We were plowing through waves steeper than any I had ever seen before.

I stared openmouthed in horror at the mountainous swell that loomed above us. Up, and up, and up the *Morning Star* rose, hesitating for a split second at its crest, then plunging forward to slide down into the trough, where she fetched up with a violent, bone-cracking shudder that boomed like thunder and shook the deck beneath our feet.

Another tremendous wave broke over the bow and swept across the deck, soaking us where we stood. I shrieked and Papa, who was struggling alongside Long Tom to hold the wheel steady, turned and caught sight of us in the doorway. His face paled.

"Get below!" he bellowed. "Sprigg! Blast you,

Sprigg, where are you? Keep these children below!"

From the pinched look on Sprigg's face as he hustled us back down the stairs, I was sure we were in for a proper thumping. The fact that he merely plucked our wet cloaks from us and whisked us into our stateroom, saying shakily that he was sorry there'd be no hot bricks tonight, as the captain had ordered all fires put out on account of the storm, filled me with sudden foreboding.

Thaddeus was oblivious to the danger, of course, leaping about and squealing as the *Morning Star* bucked like a mad horse. Sprigg finally wrestled him into his bunk and got him to promise—after threatening to tie him in—that he would lie still.

"Would you like me to stay here with you two tonight, Miss Patience?" he offered, in an anxious and most un-Sprigglike tone.

"Oh, we'll be all right, I think," I replied.

Sprigg eyed me, unconvinced. "I'll bid you good night, then," he said. "I'm needed up on deck."

It was pitch black in our stateroom without Sprigg's lantern, and the storm which raged outside seemed infinitely more terrifying in the darkness. Eyes squeezed shut, I lay rigidly in my bunk with the quilts pulled up to my chin, grateful for the wooden latticework that kept me from being flung to the floor with each heave of the ship.

From all sides, the wind shrieked and howled like a banshee. Rain lashed against the windows in Papa's day cabin, which rattled and shook as the tempest unleashed its fury. I could hear water rushing down the companionway stairs and through the grating in the day cabin floor, sloshing into our stateroom and then out again as the *Morning Star* floundered in the tumultuous swell.

I pulled the quilts over my head.

"Mama!" I said, softly so as not to alarm my little brother. I had never missed her more than I did at that moment, and I longed with all my heart for the comfort of her presence and the reassuring touch of her hand.

Over the past months I had come to think of the *Morning Star* as a fine ship, but she seemed fragile to me now, a feeble, paltry thing whose oak planking—all that separated us from the frenzy of the elements outside—was suddenly very frail indeed.

I thought of Papa and Cousin Jeremiah, of the mates and the idlers—not so idle tonight!—and Big John and Charlie Fishback and all the others up there, bravely battling the gale, and I whispered a prayer for their safety.

And one for my own as well, as I huddled in the dark, vainly trying to imagine that I was safe in bed at home. Fortunate indeed were those ashore on Nantucket and elsewhere tonight, spared from the terrors of a tempest at sea.

"Patience?" my brother called.

I poked my head out from beneath the covers. "Yes, Tad?"

"Does Papa like storms?"

"Oh, I'm sure he doesn't mind them," I lied.

"Do they frighten him?"

"Not at all."

"Then I'm not frightened either," he said stoutly.

"That's the spirit!" I told him. "You're a Goodspeed through and through."

We both grew quiet again. Though Thaddeus said he wasn't afraid, I was—more afraid than I had ever been in my life, and when the door to our stateroom banged open a few minutes later I jumped up and screamed, certain that the *Morning Star* was coming apart at her seams.

It was only Papa, however.

"Papa!" I cried in relief.

He held his lantern aloft and looked at us, tight lipped. He was soaked to the skin, and water streamed from his hair and beard and mackintosh. His eyes met mine for a long moment, and the question I so desperately wanted to ask him died on my lips.

I wanted to hear him say that all would be well, that the storm would pass and we would be safe, and that we would not perish here, tonight, in these wild, forsaken seas half a world away from home. But he turned and left without another word, banging the door shut behind him.

I burrowed my head beneath my quilt again and began to cry.

January 3, 1836

The storm raged for five days. Five fearsome days in which we were flogged by howling winds and rain and blasted by waves that threatened to swallow us whole. The nights were the worst— long, dark, and interminable—but the Morning Star *is a sturdy ship, and we survived.*

We are much battered and bruised, however, and are now limping north again along the coast of Chile for Valparaiso, where we'll put in for repairs, Papa says.

Christmas came and went without so much as a by-your-leave, as did New Year's Day, though Papa has promised we shall have a proper celebration once we reach port. This morning I passed out my taffy to the crew, who thanked me kindly, but even that did not lift our spirits.

We are sadly diminished in number and strength, I fear. Long Tom slipped from an icy shroud on the last night of the storm and was tossed into the sea. There was nothing anyone could do for him, Papa says regretfully.

I am sure he is right, but oh! how we all shall miss Long Tom's cheerful smile, and especially his music!

And there's more bad news as well, for Cousin Jeremiah has broken his leg.

—P.

Eleven

The earth has guilt, the earth has care;
Unquiet are its graves.
But peaceful sleep is ever there
Beneath the dark blue waves.

—*The Ocean*

In addition to his duties as master of the ship, Papa was responsible for doctoring the crew, and so to him fell the task of mending Cousin Jeremiah's leg, at least until we could reach Valparaiso and have it seen to properly.

We'd had our share of small mishaps thus far on our voyage—the odd splinter and bruise, a sore tooth that had to be pulled, and Doyle suffered a nasty burn when he pitched a piece of blubber into the try-pot too vigorously and got his arm splashed with hot oil—but this was far more severe. Papa had to dose Cousin Jeremiah with laudanum for the pain, and he looked grim every time he emerged from the tiny stateroom where our first mate lay pale and motionless in his bunk.

Papa had yet another bleak task to carry out now that we were safely beyond the storm, that of Long Tom's funeral service. Shortly after breakfast Mr. Chase called all hands, and we gathered by the mainmast, where Papa began by reading a passage from Psalms:

> *"They that go down to the sea in ships, that do*
> *business in great waters;*
> *These see the works of the Lord, and his*
> *wonders in the deep.*
> *For he commandeth, and raiseth the stormy wind,*
> *which lifteth up the waves thereof.*
> *He maketh the storm a calm, so that the waves*
> *thereof are still.*
> *Then are they glad because they be quiet; so he*
> *bringeth them unto their desired haven."*

After he had finished, he closed his black leather Bible and gazed solemnly around at the assembled ship's company.

"Thomas Gunnarson was a God-fearing man and a fine sailor," Papa said. "He always did his duty, worked hard, and didn't complain. He was ready with a kind word and a helping hand for those less fortunate than himself, and in that he stands as an example to us all."

He paused and gave a short nod to Mr. Macy, who stepped forward clutching a piece of paper in his hand. Our third mate fancied himself a bit of a poet, and often treated us to his latest inspiration over dinner. Clearing his throat, he began.

"As I was Long Tom's watch officer, I felt it appropriate to pen a verse in his honor." His voice broke nervously on the last word, which ended in a squeak. There was a stifled guffaw from the knot of men before him.

"It's Bunion and Toad," whispered Thaddeus.

Sure enough, as Papa looked sharply around for the culprits, I saw Binyon nudge Todd, who quickly wiped the smirk off his face.

"Weasels," I said under my breath.

Mr. Macy cleared his throat again and started to read:

> *"The sea curls o'er him, and the foaming billow*
> *As his head now rests, upon a watery pillow;*
> *But the spirit divine, has ascended to rest,*
> *To mingle with those, who are ransomed and blest."*

It was a simple sentiment, but well put, and a low murmur of approval went up from the crew. Papa then called for anyone else to step forward who wanted to say a few words, and many did so, a testament to Long Tom's popularity with his shipmates.

As there was no body to commit to the waves, Papa closed with the Twenty-third Psalm, and then Big John stepped forward with the dead man's sea chest.

"All right, men, gather round," Mr. Chase said.

"What are they doing?" Thaddeus asked.

I shrugged, and we both looked at Sprigg.

"It's tradition," he rasped. "Long Tom's gear will be auctioned off, and the money that's raised sent home to his family."

We left them to their joyless task and went below for dinner.

Later in the afternoon, we spoke the *Christopher Mitchell*, homeward bound with a full cargo of oil. Papa ordered our ship hove to for a brief gam, and exchanged the usual pleasantries about numbers of barrels taken and the price of whale oil, which Captain Harris had heard was selling for $88 a barrel in New Bedford now. Then Papa gave an account of our dreadful days rounding the Horn.

Captain Harris listened attentively, and said he hoped the weather had calmed sufficiently for him to make a more agreeable voyage himself.

"At least you'll have the wind with you," Papa said.

"Aye, there's that," Captain Harris replied. "There's nothing like battling the westerlies to put a crimp in an outward voyage."

Papa then asked if he would carry tidings of the accident to Cousin Jeremiah's wife, Lucy. "Tell her that she can write to him in Valparaiso, and that as soon as he's fit to travel, he'll be homeward bound himself."

"Valparaiso? But you're not more than a day's sail

from Talcahuano," said Captain Harris in surprise.

"Pah! That den of iniquity!" retorted Papa. "It's not worth two dead flies. No, Valparaiso it is."

Captain Harris shrugged, but promised to bring news directly to Cousin Jeremiah's wife, and we both continued on our way.

"Papa, what did you mean that Cousin Jeremiah would be homeward bound soon, too?" I asked. "His leg will heal, won't it?"

"Of course, but it's a bad break and will take months to do so properly," Papa explained. "He'd be better off ashore in the meantime, and though he could await our return from the Sandwich Islands and the Japan grounds, that seems senseless. He may as well return home to the comfort of his family."

"But how will we manage without him?"

"That, my girl, is a fine question, and one to which I am giving much thought," Papa replied. "I expect we'll find our answer in Valparaiso."

February 10, 1836

What we found in Valparaiso was Ezekiel Bridge-water.

He's our new first mate, as Mr. Chase is hopeless with navigating, despite much chewing on the end of his pencil and mopping of his brow as he sweats over his sums, and neither he nor Mr. Macy are rated as able yet. They are both much chagrined, but Papa says there's no need to be downcast, it's only common sense that we have another skilled navigator aboard. Papa says Mr. Bridgewater comes with many letters of recommendation, and is highly pleased with this turn of events. We are most fortunate to have found him, he says, but I feel Cousin Jeremiah's absence keenly.

I took an instant dislike to Mr. Bridgewater. He has the face of a ferret, with close-set eyes and a nose like the blade of a knife. His smile reveals teeth but little else, and he is as pale as the belly of a mackerel, not the usual coloring of one who earns his living at sea. He says he has been ashore due to illness, but I do not trust him. And I find it highly suspect that none of those who signed his letters of recommendation happened to be in port at the time we dropped anchor.

Nor does Mr. Bridgewater like me, of that I am sure. He observed me helping Mr. Chase solve a navigational triangle and told me in no uncertain terms to skirt off to the galley. "Little girls are unfit for men's work," he sneered, which of course did nothing to endear him to me.

Papa says I am being overly dramatic, and

that I must keep my opinions to myself, but Sprigg and Glum are stiff and unnaturally courteous in the new first mate's presence, and I don't think they like him either.

I have named him Bilgewater, and am making it my duty to keep him under close watch.

—P.

Twelve

Come all you young fellows
That's rounded the Horn,
Our captain has told us,
And we hope it will come true,
That there's plenty of sperm whales
On the coast of Peru.

—The Coast of Peru

A stretch of sweet sailing followed, as the Pacific's balmy winds blew us northward again toward the equator. For weeks we cruised the rich whaling grounds off the coasts of Chile and Peru, the tryworks regularly ablaze as our catch was turned into oil.

If I had been astounded at the size of the sperm whales we had caught previously, I was positively dumbstruck at the sight of our first right whale. Its head alone measured nearly half the length of the *Morning Star,* and it yielded far more oil than a sperm whale—some one hundred barrels—though the quality was inferior and would not fetch as great a price.

Unlike its cousin, the right whale had no teeth, but rather filtered its food through stiff strands of baleen that hung from its jaws. "Whalebone" the crew called it, and it was carefully removed and stored below, to be sold for making buggy whips, fishing rods, corset stays, and the like.

Despite the frequent bouts of arduous labor, the men were in fine spirits, buoyed as much by the splendid weather as by the success of our hunt.

"No task is too burdensome with a blue sky overhead and a fair breeze at your back," Papa said, and it was true. Glum and I made a tenuous peace in the galley, and even Sprigg was in a better temper than usual, rarely bothering to fish the thimble from his pocket to administer discipline.

After the day's work was done, there was often music, and during the dogwatch Sprigg could sometimes be persuaded to bring us up on deck to listen. Long Tom and his fiddle were sorely missed (particularly as Domingo, the Portuguese sailor who purchased the instrument at the auction, was by no means adept, and the sounds he managed to coax from it more closely resembled a wounded hound than music), but there was still Owen Gardiner on his squeezebox and Schmidt on his flute. Doyle, the Irishman, had a fine voice, well suited to the haunting ballads that he favored, and on the heartier songs we all joined in. Sprigg's singing voice was no more agreeable to listen to than his speaking voice, but Glum surprised us with a rich, deep bass that added much to the merriment.

In addition to the music, the hands loved to swap stories.

"Swapping lies is more like it," grumbled Sprigg, who added that he'd thump me for sure if he caught me repeating any of their tales—or singing any of the more colorful tunes. "Captain would have my head quicker than Jack Flash, you being nearly a young lady now and all."

Papa still made time for my navigation lessons, and I was now quite skilled at taking the noon sight with my sextant. The Pacific proved a perfect night-time classroom as well, with skies so crowded with stars that their reflection in the calm water below was like another heaven beneath us. Though we were too far south to see the North Star, still, I never failed to search for it, and thought of Mama often.

I grew daily more confident in my abilities, though I still sensed that Mr. Bridgewater did not approve of this encroachment on his territory. Papa didn't seem to notice, but there was no mistaking the wintry chill that crept into the first mate's expression whenever I emerged on deck with my sextant.

"Ah, Miss Patience!" he would cry with false delight. "Our very own mathematical genius."

I would curl my lips up in a smile as hollow as his own, and try my best to steer clear of him.

I also made sure that Ishmael kept well out of his

reach for, to add to his list of faults, Bridgewater sneezed violently whenever my little gray cat appeared.

"Blasted fleabag," he would mutter, aiming a kick at Ishmael, who thus far had nimbly avoided him.

Once we reached the latitude of the equator, we changed course and sailed due west for the Galapagos Islands. There, Papa told us, we would stop for water, fresh meat (the waters were known for their turtles, which he swore made fine eating, though I could scarce credit it), and, surprisingly, mail.

"We whalers have our own postal service," Glum informed me when I asked about this while baking cookies one afternoon.

"Really?" I said, picturing Mr. Coffin, Nantucket's own bespectacled postmaster, and the tidy brick building that housed his office.

Cheered by the prospect of gingersnaps, his favorite treat, Glum grew unusually expansive. "Nothing fancy, mind you. Just a wooden box nailed to a tree on Charles Island. Every ship stops to deliver letters she may be carrying, and check for those from folks at home."

"Do you think there will be any for us?"

The cook shrugged his narrow shoulders. "It's possible. We were delayed a bit what with the Horn and settling Mr. Folger in Valparaiso."

"I shall have to write to Aunt Anne and Martha," I said. "And Miss Mitchell, of course. Who will you write to, Glum?"

Glum's bald pate grew pink with embarrassment. He cleared his throat. "Mother would be pleased to hear from me," he mumbled.

I stared at him in astonishment. It had never occurred to me that Glum might have a mother. I felt a sudden pang as I thought of Mama. How I missed her still!

We reached our destination in less than a fortnight, our hold now boasting a full thousand barrels of oil. Papa was jubilant, for this was the most he'd taken by this point on any of his past whaling cruises. As we dropped anchor in the tiny harbor at Charles Island, he gathered the hands and announced a holiday to celebrate.

"Glum will fry up doughnuts in hot whale oil, of course—it wouldn't be a proper thousand-barrel party without them!—but we'll have turtle steaks and turtle soup to boot, and if my daughter can be persuaded, fresh biscuits and perhaps a pie or two," he said.

A cry of "Hear, hear!" went up on deck, and Papa continued, "Make haste, men, and see if you can't catch us our dinner!"

Once ashore the crew scattered to do his bidding.

Sprigg herded Thaddeus and me toward the post box, which we eagerly emptied onto the sand and knelt down to sort through.

There were a number of letters in the box, but only three for the *Morning Star.*

"Here's one for Cousin Jeremiah," I said. "Pity he's not here to enjoy it."

"Captain'll put his Valparaiso address on it and we'll tuck it back in the box," said Sprigg, plucking it out of my hand.

"Here's one for us!" cried Thaddeus, who immediately set about opening it.

The only other letter for a member of our crew was in a grimy envelope marked with waterstains and inkspots. Whereas all the other letters carried both the name of the person to whom they were addressed, and the name of their ship, this one only carried a single word: Bridgewater.

I handed it to Sprigg, who held it gingerly by the corner, as if something unsavory might crawl out from underneath the flap and bite him.

"And who'd be wanting to write to that slimy bit o' seaweed?" he muttered, grimacing.

"Why Sprigg, I thought you were fond of our first mate," I said with an innocent smile.

He snorted and cast me a sour look, then, after extracting a promise from me to keep a close eye on

Thaddeus, left us in the shade with our letters, and returned to the whaleboat where Big John was waiting to ferry him back to the ship.

"Martha has written us, and there's a letter for each of us from Aunt Anne!" said Thaddeus, who had finally managed to pry open the envelope.

I patted the sand beside me. "Come sit by me, Tad, and we'll read them together."

He obeyed. "Read Martha's first," he said.

"Very well. 'Dear Children,'" I began. "'It's awfully quiet here without you. Patches and I rattle around the house like two dried peas in a bucket. We hardly know what to do without you. I still think your father should have left you here with me, but seeing as how he didn't, I pray that the good Lord keeps you safe. I hope that you are minding your father and staying out of trouble. Your loving Martha. P.S. I've already planned the feast I'll serve upon your homecoming, and have invited Fanny Starbuck, who sends her best and particularly asks to be remembered to your father.'"

I smiled ruefully. The letter sounded just like our housekeeper, and I was struck with a pang of homesickness.

"Now Aunt Anne's," prodded Thaddeus.

I opened up the envelope that was addressed to him. "'Dear Thaddeus,'" I read.

My brother's face split into a wide smile. "I've never had a letter all of my own before," he said.

"Hush now, and listen to what it says," I replied, and began again. "'Dear Thaddeus, I hope this letter finds you in good health. By now you have rounded the Horn and reached the Pacific Ocean. How glorious! I trust you are being a good boy, and minding Patience and your papa. Please write and tell me all about your adventures. Your affectionate Aunt Anne.'"

I looked up. Thaddeus was still smiling.

"Well, there you are," I said.

He reached for the piece of paper and examined it closely, then folded it carefully and tucked it into the pocket of his trousers. "Will you help me write to them later?" he asked.

"Of course."

"And now can I go and play?"

"May I," I corrected. "Yes, if you stay right here on the beach where I can see you."

He nodded and scurried off toward the water's edge. I watched him for a moment, then opened my own letter from Aunt Anne.

"Dear Patience," she wrote. "How I wish I could be with you when you read this! You're likely sitting on some fair tropical isle with the sun shining brightly upon you, while I'm mired in the snow and ice of a New England winter. Boston seems

interminably dull after my time with you all on Nantucket, and though the school must needs be tended to, I find that I chafe at being anchored to my desk. My pupils would be scandalized to discover that though her body stands before them at the blackboard, their headmistress's thoughts often escape the confines of the classroom, passing through the window, across the city, and down to the harbor, from whence they drift readily out to sea. I often wonder about all the new places you and your papa and brother will explore, and all the new experiences that await you, and have taken to poring over my atlas in a vain attempt to imagine where you might be. I do hope that the journal I sent along has inspired you to keep a record of all that happens, as I will be eager to hear every detail. Please write me at your earliest opportunity. I long to hear that you are safe and happy. Your affectionate Aunt Anne."

It was a most satisfactory letter, and I was just beginning to reread it when there was a whoop from the shore. I looked up to see my brother seated on the back of an enormous tortoise.

"Thaddeus!" I screamed, leaping to my feet. I stuffed Aunt Anne's letter into the pocket of my pinafore and raced toward him.

"Look, Patience!" he cried happily, waving his

cap. "It's just like riding Matthew Starbuck's pony back home!"

"Get down this instant," I cried. "That beast could be dangerous!"

"Chips says they're not. And besides, look at the others."

He pointed down the beach. My mouth dropped open as I spied half the crew of the *Morning Star*, including Charlie Fishback, seated on the backs of a number of the creatures, while the other half looked on and hollered encouragement.

The frolic continued for a while, and then Big John reappeared in the whaleboat. I finally managed to pull Thaddeus off his unusual steed, and he stood beside me and watched wistfully as it lumbered away.

He tugged on my sleeve. "Patience, do you think Papa would let me keep one as a pet?"

I laughed. "He might let you bring it aboard, but not as a pet," I replied. "I'm afraid Papa and Glum have other plans for these creatures. Come along now; we'd best not keep Big John waiting. I've got pies and biscuits to make."

May 5, 1836

The one-thousand-barrel feast was a success. Despite my misgivings, the turtle meat indeed proved delicious, and we all stuffed ourselves until we couldn't eat another bite. My own contributions to the meal were gladly received, and the crew even struck up a song in my honor.

For the past few days we have been busy taking on fresh water and turtles, whose meat will help keep us until we reach the Sandwich Islands. They are the perfect livestock for a sailing ship, Papa says, as they can survive a long time without food or water. Thaddeus has taken a great liking to them, and can frequently be found in the hold where they are kept. Sometimes he lugs one of the smaller ones back up on deck for sport.

We have spent a great deal of time ashore, and despite the frequent warm rains that send us running for shelter, Thaddeus and I have seen a good bit of the island. So far we have spied sea lions, penguins, and even the blue-footed booby for which these parts are so famous.

This morning I also spied something that did not please me nearly as much—Bilgewater, in close conference with Bunion and Toad. An unholy trio if ever I saw one.

I told Papa, but he merely shrugged and said, "He's their watch officer, Patience. He's bound to speak to them from time to time. You mustn't let your imagination run away with you."

Despite what he says, I am convinced that Bilgewater is up to no good. But trying to convince Papa of this is like trying to spit into a hurricane. It's simply no use.

—*P.*

Thirteen

Now when the wound the whale doth feel,
He scampers off quite quick, sir.
Perhaps he gives the boat a whack,
In pieces soon it is, sir.
Now this advice 'tis well to take
To place your iron firm, sir,
And look out sharp and keep quite clear
From fins and flukes and jaws, sir.

—*A Whaling Scene*

We were cruising the line now, heading due west at zero degrees latitude along the equator. Though the wind continued favorable, it was hot as blazes. Pitch oozed from between the planks on deck, and Papa rigged a wind sail on the quarterdeck to funnel air down the companionway to our stuffy quarters below.

Tempers began to fray with the heat. I was on the outs with Glum again, and Sprigg was in a vile humor, screeching at the slightest provocation and sending Thaddeus running to Chips for refuge. There were fisticuffs in the fo'c'sle, and Papa had to threaten the guilty parties—Domingo and another of the Azoreans, Antonio by name—with a taste of the cat-o'-nine-tails before they would finally cease.

Binyon and Todd had renewed their attacks on poor Charlie as well, and though he was their watch officer and thus responsible for their discipline, Bridgewater didn't lift a finger to stop them. Indeed, he appeared to enjoy their cruel sport, watching in amusement as Charlie, flushed in the face and miserable, was set upon like a fox by a pair of hunting dogs.

My dislike for Bridgewater grew daily. Yesterday I caught him rummaging in the drawers of Papa's desk. He started when he heard me come in, but said smoothly, "Your father sent me to fetch the *Practical Navigator.*"

I pointed wordlessly to where the book lay in plain sight, smack in the middle of the desktop.

"Ah," he replied with one of his thin smiles. "How could I have overlooked it?"

How indeed, I wondered, but held my tongue.

June 9, 1836

Bilgewater knows I dislike him.

He is a bit of a dandy, and likes nothing better than to take his watch on deck, his chest puffed out with importance as he struts back and forth, calling orders to the men. He is also very particular about his clothing, and even at the dinner table his fingers unconsciously fuss about his person, smoothing his hair or his neckerchief, or fiddling with his buttons.

He caught me mimicking him to Thaddeus the other day, rounding the mizzenmast unexpectedly as I pranced and preened. Now he watches me closely, a thoughtful expression on his face, and he has taken to paying me extravagant compliments. I cannot fathom his reason for this, unless it is an attempt to curry favor with Papa.

"Why if it isn't Miss Patience!" he cries in false delight as I appear to help take the noon sighting. "The Morning Star's cleverest crew member!" Or, helping himself to a third slice of pie—he is a glutton—"Miss Patience, I'd wager this pie is the finest I've ever eaten."

He is as slippery as an eel in a barrel of oil, and I am having none of it.

—P.

On a clear, bright morning midmonth we had a brush with disaster.

A pod of whales was sighted shortly after breakfast, and the boats quickly lowered away. As had become our habit, Thaddeus and I stood at the siderail of the *Morning Star* on overturned buckets to watch the hunt. Sprigg kept a close eye on us now whenever the boats were away, and we had not been able to repeat our climb to the masthead.

Mr. Chase's boat was in the lead, his crew pulling hard, and right upon his heels were Papa and Mr. Bridgewater, while Mr. Macy took up the rear.

Kanaka Jim was Mr. Chase's boatsteerer, and once he planted his harpoon in the broad black back of the nearest whale, he and Mr. Chase began to trade places, as was customary. Hardly had they begun, however, when the injured whale threw himself up in the air—"breaching" they call it—and fell back into the water with a mighty splash that set the small boat to rocking wildly.

The creature then dove, only to reappear again a few seconds later directly under them. The force of his surfacing cracked the boat in two like an egg, sending men flying into the air in every direction.

Papa and the others were backing their boats for all they were worth in an attempt to avoid the thrashing creature, but when the whale then dashed his tail in fury against the water, the tip of it caught Papa's boat and stove it in as well.

I screamed and clutched Thaddeus's arm.

"Where's Papa?" I cried. "I can't see Papa!"

All was confusion. The whale's convulsions roiled the surface of the ocean, engulfing the men from the two wrecked boats as they swam for their lives. I watched in terror, scarce able to breathe.

Finally the injured creature took off, dragging what remained of Mr. Chase's empty boat behind him, and Bridgewater and Mr. Macy maneuvered their boats to pick up the men in the water.

We were very fortunate, as it transpired. No one was killed, though Mr. Chase banged his head severely, knocking himself senseless in the process, and surely would have drowned had it not been for his boatsteerer, who himself suffered a sprained ankle. Domingo and Antonio, fresh from their scuffle on deck, both required bandaging about the legs, and there were a host of other scrapes and bruises as well, including a nasty wound just beneath Schmidt's eye. The worst damage was to Big John, however, who broke his wrist when he was thrown heavily on the gunwale of Papa's boat.

Papa himself escaped harm, much to my great relief, and spent the remainder of the day doctoring the crew. We were much shorthanded when he was done, with all the invalids confined to their bunks until further notice. The *Morning Star* seemed strangely quiet, and only Bridgewater and Mr. Macy joined us at the table for dinner.

"We have much to be thankful for," said Papa, after he gave the blessing. "The Almighty has indeed spared us today."

We all nodded in agreement. The accident had rattled me, however, and Papa must have seen my long face for he hastened to assure me, "We'll be right as rain in a day or two, mark my word, Patience."

Fourteen

Then huzzah for a life of war and strife,
Oh, the pirate's life for me.
My bark shall ride the foaming tide,
For I am demon of the sea.

—*The Demon of the Sea*

Unfortunately a day was all it took for Bridgewater to show his true colors.

He struck late the following morning, shortly after we changed course and veered northwest for the Sandwich Islands.

Thaddeus and I had heard much about these fabled tropical isles, with their warm blue waters and white beaches, their exotic birds and animals and luscious fruits, from coconuts and breadfruits to bananas and pineapples, all of which I longed to see and taste. I was seated at Papa's desk, supposedly working a navigation problem he had set me, but instead gazing dreamily at the chart and tracing our route with my finger, when I heard the first shot.

Ishmael, who was curled up in my lap, started at the sound and flattened his ears against his head.

"Hush, Ishmael," I said, patting him soothingly. "It's only Chips banging about on deck."

The second shot was unmistakable, however. I sat bolt upright, and listened for a moment to the shouts and thuds and pounding footsteps above me. Setting my cat down, I started for the companionway and ran smack into Thaddeus, who was being hustled to safety by Sprigg.

"Get back into the cabin, Miss Patience!" he cried. "Bolt the door!"

"Why?" I asked in alarm. "What is it, Sprigg?"

"It's that blasted Bridgewater. He's taken the ship!"

I looked at him, stunned. "Bilgewater? Why on earth would he do such a thing? What does he want with the *Morning Star*? And where's Papa?"

"Did he hurt my Papa?" Thaddeus's voice was shrill.

Sprigg pushed us bodily into Papa's cabin and pulled the door shut. "No more questions from either of you. Bolt the door and stay put until I return."

It was pure torture, not knowing what was happening. I opened the stern windows, and Thaddeus and I knelt on the sofa, our faces pressed against the netting as we strained to make sense of the confusion above. The tumult on deck was deafening. I heard the clang of metal on metal, followed by hoarse shouts, another pistol shot, then silence.

Finally we heard Papa.

"Put that pistol down, Bridgewater!" he bellowed in his Cape Horn voice.

"You're hardly in a position to be giving orders, Captain," the first mate replied with an audible sneer. "Now I suggest you tell the men to cooperate, or it will be the worse for you, not to mention that pair of brats you had the misfortune to bring along."

Thaddeus crept a little closer at this, and I put my arm around him and gave him a reassuring squeeze.

"You needn't worry, Tad," I whispered. "Papa won't let anyone hurt us, especially not Bilgewater."

The first mate's voice floated down to us again. "Binyon! Todd! Drive those men forward into the fo'c'sle and chain the hatch shut!"

Bunion and Toad! I might have known those two reptiles would be involved in this.

Shortly there were footsteps on the companion-way stairs, and then someone pounded on the door.

"Open up!"

It was Binyon.

"I shan't," I replied hotly.

"You open this door now, or I'll break it down."

Reluctantly I obeyed. Binyon grabbed Thaddeus by the arm, and giving me a rough shove said, "Up on deck with you. Captain Bridgewater's orders."

So it was *Captain* Bridgewater now, I thought in disgust. What brazenness!

The first mate was standing by the mainmast, his pistol trained on Papa and the idlers. Their hands were tied behind them. The *Morning Star* looked deserted; the remainder of the crew had obviously been herded down into the fo'c'sle, from which could be heard muffled shouts and threats, punctuated by occasional bursts of thumping on the underside of the hatch. Todd lounged atop it, a razor-sharp cutting spade in his hand.

"I see you've come to join us," Bridgewater said. "Perhaps you'd care to stand by your father, and make the family portrait complete."

A low growl rumbled out of Papa's throat as we crossed the deck and took our places by his side.

"You'd do well to keep my children out of this," he warned.

Bridgewater ignored him.

"Binyon," he said, jerking his pistol aft. "You'll find a letter beneath my mattress. Bring it to me."

I looked at Sprigg, who arched an eyebrow. It could only be the letter we had retrieved from Charles Island, which in turn could only mean that Bridgewater had been scheming for quite some time, if not since before he even boarded the *Morning Star*. But what did the letter contain?

Bridgewater didn't keep us wondering long. When Binyon returned with the envelope, the first mate took it from his hand and removed the contents, unfolding what appeared to be a chart of some sort. He studied it for a long moment, then tucked it inside his jacket and said crisply, "Right. Todd, you take the wheel, and set us a course east-southeast. Binyon, we'll need to send two men aloft—fetch me that pair of hot-tempered jacks malingering in steerage."

"Domingo and Antonio?"

"Aye."

Binyon nodded, and returned shortly with the men in tow. They were both limping, and appeared greatly confused at the sight that met them as they emerged on deck. They were quick to recognize a firearm, however, and wincing, climbed awkwardly into the rigging when Bridgewater pointed his pistol at them.

Slowly the *Morning Star* responded to the reins of helm and sail and began to veer in the new direction.

"I don't know what you're about here, Bridgewater, but you'll be held accountable if I have to come back from the grave and see to it myself," said Papa.

The first mate's lips peeled back in one of his humorless smiles. "I would be delighted to give you that opportunity, Captain Goodspeed," he replied.

It was a long day. Bridgewater offered us no further explanation, but simply held the *Morning Star* to her new course. He took the noon sight by himself, nodding in satisfaction at the sextant reading, and it wasn't until late in the afternoon that he finally untied Glum and sent him into the galley, Todd at his heels to guard him with the cutting spade.

We were served a rough meal of salt beef and hardtack, and allowed a dipperful of water each. The men in the fo'c'sle received nothing, nor did the wounded in steerage.

"Is it your intention to keep us here all night?" demanded Papa.

Again Bridgewater ignored him. Thaddeus finally fell asleep across Papa's lap, and though weary and heartily discouraged, I determined to remain awake a while longer.

"How did he get the guns?" I whispered to Papa.

"He must have taken the key to the storeroom from my desk," he murmured in reply.

I thought back to the other morning, when I had caught Bridgewater in Papa's day cabin. If only I had guessed what he was about, I might have been able to prevent this.

"What does he plan to do with us?"

"I don't know, my girl," said Papa. "But he can't stay awake all night. At some point he'll close his eyes, and when he does, I'll be ready."

"As will I," murmured Chips.

"And I," said Glum. Sprigg and Owen Gardiner, the cooper, both grunted their assent as well, and bolstered by their show of spirit, I finally allowed myself to fall into a fitful slumber.

Papa was wrong, as it turned out. Bridgewater could stay awake all night and did, though the lack of sleep didn't improve his temper.

When the first glimmer of sunlight woke me, it was not, as I had hoped, to find Papa back in charge of the *Morning Star* and Bridgewater locked in irons. We were still huddled about the mainmast, the first mate's pistol trained upon us unwaveringly.

Though his eyes were now red-rimmed, Bridgewater hadn't moved a muscle all night, Papa reported under his breath. It was a disheartening turn of events.

For several hours the *Morning Star* plowed serenely onward, the gentle seas washing quietly alongside. The sun was shining brightly, and a flock of clouds as fat as the sheep on Nantucket common grazed on an endless expanse of blue sky overhead. It would have been a peaceful scene, had I not felt a chill of foreboding. What was to become of us?

"Land ho!" came a cry from above, and Bridgewater sprang to his feet.

"Where away?" he called.

"Dead ahead!"

The first mate nodded in satisfaction. "Bring us in, Mr. Todd."

We drew closer to what was soon revealed to be a small island, and shortly passed into a desolate cove. There we dropped anchor. I gazed with apprehension at the stretch of rocky beach that lay opposite. The vegetation was sparse, and it hardly resembled the kind of tropical paradise of which I had heard so many tales.

"Do you know this place, Papa?" I asked.

He shook his head.

"Quiet," snapped Bridgewater. "Into the waist boat, all of you."

A sudden hush fell across the deck, and Papa's face grew pale.

"You would maroon us?" he said, incredulous.

Marooning was one of the cruelest fates to which a sailor could be consigned. I'd heard tales of wicked captains who would set an unruly hand or two ashore with no food or water, sailing away and leaving them to their fate. If caught, the captains were punished severely, but often it was their victims who suffered the most.

If fortune smiled upon the poor souls, the isle might prove fertile, with water and meat to sustain them until the day when perchance they were spied by a passing ship. But if this were not the case, or if the barren shores were inhabited by savages—I shuddered to think of the variety of slow, painful deaths that might result.

"Not another word," barked the first mate.

Papa began to struggle then. "You will not do this!" he bellowed, and, hands still tied fast behind him, lunged toward Bridgewater, who stepped nimbly aside and stuck out his foot. Papa tripped and fell heavily, banging his head on the deck. Thaddeus began to cry.

"Papa!" I rushed to kneel by my father's side. He sat up slowly, groaning.

Ignoring my protests, Binyon and Todd lifted him bodily from the deck and dumped him unceremoniously into the whaleboat. The cooper was next, then Glum.

"The steward remains aboard to serve me," Bridgewater ordered.

He turned his attention to Chips, eyeing his strong arms and shoulders warily. "And we may need the carpenter, but I want him put in irons."

Chips bristled angrily at this. "I'm no man's slave."

"You'll be a sorry slave if you don't do as you're told," snarled Bridgewater.

"Do as he says, Chips," said Papa tonelessly.

Reluctantly Chips allowed himself to be led forward by Binyon.

"And those arrogant young pups as well," said Bridgewater, pointing to Thaddeus and me.

By now Thaddeus was howling in a mixture of anger and terror, and when Todd reached for him he bit his hand. A short scuffle ensued, but my little brother was no match for the burly sailor, and soon found himself deposited in the bottom of the whale-boat next to Glum.

Todd then turned in my direction, but suddenly Bridgewater held up his hand.

"Wait," he said, fixing me with his ferret's eyes. "I've changed my mind. She stays. I like her biscuits."

Fear gripped me and I froze, staring at him, speechless.

"My daughter comes with me," Papa said sharply.

"I beg to disagree," said Bridgewater. "I need a cook."

Glum unfolded himself slowly and stood up. "The girl can't handle the job herself," he said in his usual mournful tone.

Bridgewater eyed him with suspicion. Glum returned his gaze steadily, his face wiped clean of expression. Finally the first mate nodded. "Perhaps you're right," he said. "Out with you then."

Glum climbed from the whaleboat back onto the deck of the *Morning Star*. Warmth crept back into my veins as I caught his quick wink.

"Patience! I want Patience!" wailed Thaddeus.

I ran over to the whaleboat, and slipping my lucky silver dollar necklace over my head, passed it to my little brother. "Here Thaddeus, take this," I said. "It's good luck, and will help keep you safe."

He brightened a bit at the prospect, but before he could put it on, Binyon appeared at my elbow and plucked it out of his hand. "I'll take that," he said with a smirk. "By rights it should have been mine anyway."

"Give that back, you thief!" I fumed.

Binyon merely laughed and slung it around his neck, then shoved me back to where Sprigg and Glum were standing. We stood huddled together while the remainder of the crew was brought on deck, eyes blinking at the light after their enforced imprisonment in the fo'c'sle.

Bridgewater sorted quickly through them. All of the injured men—Big John and Mr. Chase among them—were put into the whaleboats. Then he climbed up on the main hatch and addressed the remaining hands.

"You men may choose your fate," he shouted. "You may go ashore with Captain Goodspeed, or remain aboard the *Morning Star* under my command. You'll be well paid when I sell her cargo in Talcahuano."

So he *had* been planning this all along, I thought. The greedy pig.

"You're nothing better than a common pirate!" I shouted.

Bridgewater's eyes narrowed and he turned the pistol on me. "That's quite enough out of you. Now men, make your choice!"

The crew looked bewildered.

"Is there water ashore?" cried one.

Bridgewater shrugged. "That remains to be seen, doesn't it?"

There were shouts of "blackguard!" and "ruffian!" but they were quickly quelled when Bridgewater brandished his pistol. A general shuffling of feet followed, as the men considered their options. Most determined to go with Papa, but half a dozen, including Domingo and Antonio, said they'd stay aboard.

Mr. Macy cleared his throat, looked anxiously at Papa, and squeaked, "I'll stay." Charlie Fishback, his face red with embarrassment, added that he would, too.

I looked at them both in disgust. "Traitors," I muttered under my breath.

As the men climbed into the boats, Papa staggered to his feet.

"You'll never succeed with this desperate plan," Papa said. "My ship is known in every port from here to the Arctic sea, and you'll be dragged before the law the minute the *Morning Star* is spotted."

Bilgewater laughed, a joyless sound. "Remind me not to go to the Arctic," he said. "I have friends as well, Captain Goodspeed. In fact, several are awaiting me in Talcahuano. But thank you for reminding me of one minor detail I might have overlooked. The ship's name must be changed, of course."

He stroked his chin thoughtfully. "What to call her?" he mused. His gaze fell on me.

"Of course!" he repeated with a malicious grin. "We shall call her the *Patience*. Mr. Binyon, fetch some paint from the locker aft and make it so. And take this chit below and lock her in her cabin."

Fifteen

And tell your hearts to be as one
And all your veins be free,
To fight and rather bleed and die
Than lose our liberty.

—A New Liberty Song

Rage welled up within me as Binyon pushed me roughly into Papa's day cabin. I whirled around and grabbed the doorhandle, pulling with all my might. I could hear him laughing as he fastened it shut from the outside.

Rage fueled my fists as I beat them against the door. "Let me out this minute, Bunion!" I cried.

He merely laughed again.

"You sorry son of a blackfish!" I said.

The laughing stopped. "You hold your tongue, minx, or I will unlock the door, and then we'll see who's sorry!"

I delivered a final kick to the door and retreated.

The rage subsided, leaving in its wake a cold fury. I would not sit here and do nothing while that vermin Bridgewater carried out his plan. But what could I do? The minutes ticked by, and as I glanced around the cabin, considering the possibilities, I thought of what Papa had said long ago, when we first began our voyage. What was it? *A ship's crew is like a family,* he had said, and something about each one's particular abilities being needed. *We're stronger together than when we work alone,* he had said too. But what were my abilities?

My gaze fell on Papa's pocket watch, which lay on his desk where he had left it. Idly I checked the time. It was nearly noon. Suddenly I had an idea. Dropping the watch into my pinafore pocket, I raced into our stateroom, where I snatched up my sextant and thrust it into my other pocket. I might not be able to stop Bridgewater from marooning Papa and Thaddeus and the others, but I could certainly see to it that we would find them again.

Hurrying back into Papa's cabin, I rattled the door handle one more time. Still locked. In frustration, I turned around and leaned against the door. The Tad-Catcher caught my eye. Of course! I listened closely for a moment, but there were no sounds from the other side of the door. Binyon must have returned on deck to join his fellow mutineers.

Climbing up on the sofa, I heard Bridgewater give the order to lower the first whaleboat. There was no time to be lost! Moving swiftly now, I began to pull desperately at the netting. Chips had fastened it well, and it didn't budge. Panic welled up in me, and I ran to Papa's desk and rummaged through the drawers for something sharp, finally emerging with his letter opener.

As I began to saw at the netting, Thaddeus's high voice rang out above the squealing of the davits.

"My Papa will make you pay for this, Bilgewater!"

A shout of laughter went up from the crew as they heard our pet name for Bridgewater for the first time.

"That's *Mr.* Bilgewater to you, Tad," Papa boomed, and I was heartened to hear the spirit in his voice again.

"Hold your tongues! All of you!" screeched Bridgewater. "Not another word out of any of you!"

The last of the netting finally gave way, and clambering onto the sill, I glanced down at the water below me. It was impossibly clear, and I could see all the way to the bottom. A long shadow flitted across the sand—a shark? I didn't wait to find out, but quickly removed my shoes and tucked my skirt and petticoat and pinafore into my pantaloons—thankful there was no one nearby to see me. Balancing precariously, I stretched upwards. By standing on my tiptoes I could just reach the bottom of the taffrail.

I hauled myself up as quietly as possible and dropped onto the deck. Peeping around the wheel, I could just see Bridgewater, who stood to the side as his traitorous assistants lowered the second boat to the water.

"Handsomely now, Mr. Todd! Steady as she goes!"

Moving swiftly out of sight behind the deckhouse, I lost no time in directing the eyepiece of my sextant toward the horizon. My hands were shaking, and I willed them to be still. I took a series of readings, as

Papa had shown me, glancing at his pocket watch after each one until I was certain that the sun had reached its zenith. I committed the numbers to memory, and risked another glance forward.

There was a splash as the third boat dropped into the water, and then Bridgewater sneezed.

"Where is that blasted cat?" he hollered. "I want it off this ship once and for all!"

Ishmael! I held my breath, praying that my cat would once again avoid the first mate's clutches.

"There you are, you little wretch," he said. "Come here! You're going overboard as well!"

I heard scuffling noises followed by a sharp meow, then a curse and a thud, as if something had been dropped onto the deck.

Peeking around the wheel again, I saw Bridgewater nursing his hand. Ishmael must have bitten him.

"Shall I have a go at it, Cap'n?" asked Todd.

"Never mind about the cat for now," Bridgewater snapped. "Cut them away, Mr. Binyon!"

The sun glinted on Binyon's knife. He sliced the lines and flung them into the trio of whaleboats, severing the last tenuous strands that connected my father and brother to the *Morning Star.*

"You still have time to reconsider, Bridgewater," Papa called from below, but there was only laughter in reply. Then Thaddeus's voice drifted back to me. "Patience! I want Patience!" he said again.

It was all I could do not to run to him. I clenched the sextant so tightly the metal cut into my hand.

"Away with you now! Pull for shore, before I blast you ashore!" cried Bridgewater, and I heard the oars drop slowly, reluctantly into the water as the whale-boats began to make for the island.

Bridgewater turned to the small knot of silent men who remained on deck. "I am your captain now," he announced. "Unless you want the same fate or worse, you will do as I say."

I dared not linger on deck any longer, for fear I would be discovered. I dropped back over the taffrail, my bare toes feeling for the window ledge as Bridge-water gave the quick succession of orders that would send the *Morning Star* on her way.

Once back inside I untucked my skirt and petti-coat and pinafore and crossed quickly to Papa's desk. There I took his pen and wrote down the maximum sextant reading from my observations on deck. I applied the corrections from the *Practical Navigator*— the dip of the horizon caused by the height of my eye above the water, the refraction caused by the earth's atmosphere, the angular radius of the sun, the index error of my sextant—so many details to remember! Drawing Papa's watch from my pocket, I compared it to the chronometer for Greenwich time.

I must hurry! Heart thumping, I riffled through the pages of the *Nautical Almanac* to find today's date—

there!—and time—there!—and ran my finger down the column of numbers for the proper declination of the sun. Then, as Cousin Jeremiah had instructed me, I swiftly calculated our latitude.

I wrote down the result—2°40' S—and carefully committed it to memory. I could only hope and pray that, armed with this tiny shred of information, I might be able to find Papa and Thaddeus again.

The floor tilted beneath me as the wind caught the sails and the *Morning Star* began to swing around toward the open sea. I stared blindly at the numbers in my hand for a moment, then thrust the paper into my pocket and crossed to the window. In the distance I could see Papa and Thaddeus standing on the shore with their band of faithful crew members.

I took my handkerchief out and waved it furiously.

"Papa!" I cried, knowing that my words could not be heard above the surf. Tears blinded me, and I blinked fiercely, struggling to keep my father and brother in view. Oh, Aunt Anne was right, the ties that bound us together were fragile, and I thought my heart would break as I felt them ripping apart. "I love you, Papa! I love you, Thaddeus! I will come back for you!"

After a moment I saw an answering flutter of white. Papa had seen me! I continued to wave, as did he, our handkerchiefs signaling our hearts, until long after the tiny island passed out of sight.

Sixteen

The stars are rushing by us now,
As scattered by the blast,
Now all the shores are vanishing,
Now all the islands past.

—*Most Beautiful*

June 15, 1836

Overnight the Morning Star has become my prison.

Bilgewater may have kept me aboard, but he certainly does not mean for my life to continue as usual. He has taken over our quarters, and I have been moved to Cousin Jeremiah's tiny stateroom. I am kept locked in, except for brief periods of freedom, belowdecks mostly.

"Bad for morale was the crew to see you," Bilgewater says with a nasty smile.

Not that he lets his qualms about morale stand in the way when he wishes to fill his belly. Biscuits and pies, doughnuts, cookies and cakes—there seems to be no end to his greed. Glum grumbles that he has turned our ship into a floating bakeshop, and says at this rate we will *run out of stores well before we reach Talcahuano.*

I have not spoken a single word to Bilgewater since he set Papa and Thaddeus ashore, nor will I. He is beneath contempt. I have spent countless hours over the past days dreaming up elaborate retributions for his traitorous acts. Hanging is too good for him, I have concluded. I would far rather feed him to the sharks, or boil him slowly in oil over the tryworks. Better yet, lash him to a whale and give him a Nantucket sleigh ride straight to the devil himself.

It is hot and airless in this cabin, and I have nothing to do but write in my journal and read. Worse, with nothing to engage it, my mind whirls with anxiety for Papa and Thaddeus. What is to be their fate? What if there is no water on the island? Or what if savages lurk on its rocky shores?

I fear I will go mad with worry and boredom.

—P.

Days passed, and above me the life of the ship followed a semblance of its normal routine, the bell clanging at its usual intervals to mark the changing of the watch. With each passing hour we drew further and further from Papa and Thaddeus—surely hundreds of miles of ocean separated us by now—and I grew more and more disheartened.

Chips appeared shortly after I was moved to Cousin Jeremiah's cabin, a wary and well-armed Binyon on hand to stand guard as he cut a small opening in the bottom of my door.

As he sawed, Chips glanced up at me and smiled.

"You bearing up all right, Miss Patience?" he asked in a low voice.

I nodded. "I guess so."

"You're here to work, not for a gam," said Binyon loudly, fingering my silver dollar.

Chips finished with his saw, then straightened up and turned toward the man behind him. Though Binyon was tall, Chips towered over him. There was a menacing edge to his voice.

"'Taint right to keep a young one penned up like this," he growled. "You ought to be ashamed."

Binyon reddened and took a step backward, then he jerked his pistol toward the companionway. "Away with you now," he said.

Chips moved reluctantly, and Binyon slammed my door shut, locking it again.

The purpose for the hole at the base of my door soon became clear, as plates of food began appearing through it at mealtimes. Glum and Sprigg saw to it that I didn't starve, though I suspected that Binyon and Todd helped themselves to the choicer bits before delivering my meals.

The opening had another advantage, as it allowed Ishmael to visit, and I was much cheered by his company, though still fearful that he would run afoul of Bridgewater.

The hole at the bottom of my door also enabled me to hear the conversation at the dinner table. Bridgewater was always careful to leave either Binyon or Todd on deck at mealtime, bristling with pistols, but whoever wasn't standing watch was allowed to join him below, as was Mr. Macy, with whom he was clearly trying to ingratiate himself.

"Another slice of pork roast, Mr. Macy?" he would say in his unctuous voice.

"If you'd be so kind, Mr. Bridgewater," the third mate would squeak in reply. In my mind's eye, I could just see his Adam's apple bobbing nervously, the rat.

On the afternoon of the fifth day after the mutiny, I was lying on Cousin Jeremiah's bunk in a listless stupor. I thought I heard light footsteps descending the companionway stairs, but ignored them. It was only Bridgewater, more than likely.

There was a quick tap on my door.

"Miss Patience!" someone called softly.

I sat up. I knew that voice.

"You may as well go back up on deck, Charlie Fishback," I whispered furiously. "I don't speak to scrubs like you."

There was a pause, and he cleared his throat.

"I don't know what they told you, but I ain't no scrub, Miss Patience," he said. "I stayed aboard because I thought I could help you."

"You're a poor liar," I replied.

"Ask Glum, he'll—"

There was a loud thud, and then Binyon bellowed, "Get back on deck, farmboy, or I'll hang you from the rigging by your thumbs!"

I didn't hear any more from Charlie that day, but I did manage to speak to Glum later, when Bridgewater had me brought up to help in the galley.

"Charlie told me he stayed aboard in hopes of being of assistance," I muttered under my breath, passing him a tray of cookies to put in the oven.

Glum glanced sharply over my shoulder, where Todd was lounging by the skylight. Bridgewater had forbidden us from talking together while we worked.

He gave a quick nod.

"So did Mr. Macy," he whispered.

My heart beat a little faster when I heard this. "That makes four, counting you and Sprigg—no, five, there's Chips as well! What about the others?"

Glum opened the stove door with a clatter and leaned over, the top of his bald head gleaming in the heat. His mouth was inches from my ear. "They'll swing with the prevailing wind. If we can take the upper hand, they'll side with us."

"What do we do now?" I asked.

"Lie low and await the right moment," he murmured, as he shut the stove door closed again with a clang.

Easy enough for him to say, I thought ruefully, stoic that he was. It was an altogether different matter for me, however, as heaven only knew what an impatient creature I was. Plus, it was my family who was in grave danger, not his.

Todd looked over at us. "'Ere, what are you two nattering about. You know the captain's orders," he said, crossing to the galley.

I thrust a plate of cookies under his nose and gave him my most innocent smile. "Would you like a gingersnap?" I said.

Seventeen

Cheer up, cheer up, my lively lads;
Let not your courage fail,
For Providence will have her way.
Let a man do all he can, brave boys,
Let a man do all he can.

—*The Whalefish Song*

Late into the night I paced the floor of my cabin. There must be something I could do to help us take the *Morning Star* back, but what?

My gaze fell on the sea chest tucked under my bunk. Bridgewater had allowed me to bring my possessions along to Cousin Jeremiah's cabin, and I had haphazardly grabbed whatever came to hand—my journal, of course, along with my sextant, some clothing, the quilts Mama made us, a few books, and my doll, Miranda. Hidden beneath Miranda's dress, wound safely around her waist, was Mama's precious strand of pearls. It would never do for Bridgewater to catch sight of those! Now it occurred to me that there might be something else of use inside, and a hazy plan began to form in my mind.

Kneeling down I pulled the wooden trunk from its stowage spot and lifted the lid. But as I pawed through its jumbled contents, I discovered that what I sought was missing. I must have left it behind in Papa's day cabin.

"Blast that infernal Bilgewater!" I said crossly to Ishmael, who was curled up on my bunk. He slitted an eye and regarded me with sleepy curiosity. How was I to get it back? I was never out of sight of Binyon or Todd, and even if I did manage to slip away, if they caught me rummaging through Papa's things, there'd be the devil to pay.

"We'll just have to risk it, won't we," I told my cat.

I grabbed my pen and tore a sheet of paper out of my journal. As I jotted down instructions for Charlie Fishback, it suddenly occurred to me that he might not be able to read. I knew that Glum and Sprigg could, but it wasn't their watch, and they were most likely asleep. And if Bilgewater got ahold of my note! I quailed at the thought and started to crumple the paper, then stopped. I could conceive of no other way to achieve my goal. As it was, success would require nerves of steel, the cooperation of all of us, and more than our fair share of luck.

Hastily folding the note and tucking it into my pocket, I crossed to the door and began banging on it wildly. As I had hoped, it didn't take long for someone to respond.

"'Ere now, what's all this racket?" said Todd in a querulous voice.

"I need to use the privy!"

"At this hour of the night? Ain't you gone and done that already?"

"Todd, let me out," I pleaded. "It's urgent."

Grumbling, he unlocked the door. His pistol was strapped to his waist as usual. "Blasted hen frigate," he muttered, shooing me up the companionway stairs. "Womenfolk is a nuisance at sea, everyone knows that. Why Cap'n saw fit to keep you aboard is a mystification."

As I stepped onto the deck, I looked about me quickly, hoping to spot Charlie. But there was no sign of life aside from Domingo, who was standing his trick at the helm. I was sure this was Charlie's watch! I craned my neck upwards into the rigging, but saw nothing but sky and stars.

"Mind you be quick about it now," said Todd irritably, as we reached the foredeck. I ignored him and took my time, lingering at the head—the sailors' privy at the bow of the *Morning Star*—as long as I dared. Charlie *must* be about somewhere.

Perhaps I'd have to wait until morning. But I hated to even think of that, as I knew every moment of delay took us farther and farther from Papa and Tad.

"Come on, then," said Todd, as I finally emerged from the shadows. I trailed slowly behind him.

As we passed the midship shelter, the steerage hatch slid open and Charlie's head emerged.

"There you are!" cried Todd, as he clambered out onto the deck. "You finished with that hog yet, farmboy? Captain Bridgewater won't be happy if he doesn't get 'is ham for breakfast."

Charlie nodded. "He'll have his ham."

Todd looked at me. "Let's get you back below," he said testily.

I took a deep breath. It was now or never. Palming the note, I pretended to stumble as I passed Charlie. He reached out to steady me and I grabbed his hand, squeezing it hard and pressing the note into it.

"Thank you, Charlie," I said.

Surprised, he opened his mouth to reply, then thought better of it and merely lifted his cap. Todd swiveled around and looked at the two of us suspiciously for a long moment.

"Hurry up there, missy," he said finally. "And you get on with your duties, firetop."

My heart was pounding wildly as Todd led me back to my cabin and locked me in. I felt an unaccustomed surge of hope. The note was safely transferred to Charlie! He'd kept his wits about him, and now it only remained to be seen whether he could read.

June 20, 1836

I have been awake since before dawn, nervous as a long-tailed cat in a room full of rocking chairs, as Mama used to say. Speaking of cats, Ishmael is nowhere to be seen, but he must have returned for a visit during the night as there's a fresh mouse at the foot of my bunk.

Giving it a wide berth, I dressed myself, and am now seated here with nothing to do but wait.

If my trick works, I should shortly have what I need to put my plan into action. If it doesn't, this will likely be my last diary entry, as I'll surely be flogged, or worse. I'm only sorry you aren't here to wish me luck, Aunt Anne—I could certainly use it, for I can only imagine the dire consequences if Bilgewater discovers what I intend to do.

—P.

Shortly after the first watch tumbled up from the fo'c'sle, there was a sharp cry of pain from the deck above.

I strained to listen through the rush of footsteps that passed above my cabin. Soon, as I had hoped, Binyon came for me.

"Captain Bridgewater says be quick about it," he said sourly.

Meekly I followed him to where the first mate stood near Chips's worktable. I was surprised to see Chips sitting on the deck slumped against his table, his left arm cradled in his lap. Where was Charlie?

"This careless fellow has managed to gash himself with his chisel," said Bridgewater, eyeing the wound with distaste. "I'd stitch him up myself, but it might spoil my breakfast."

I leaned over to take a better look and drew in my breath sharply. It was a nasty wound indeed. Straightening up, I looked Bridgewater in the eye. "I'll need Papa's doctoring bag," I said. I hoped my nervousness didn't show. Without Papa's bag, my plan would fail.

"Very well," said Bridgewater. He jerked his head aft. "Fetch it for her, will you, Binyon?"

As Binyon sauntered off, I crouched beside my patient. "And you'll need to unchain him," I added casually, exchanging a glance with Chips.

"Absolutely not," snapped Bridgewater.

"But I can't attend to him properly otherwise!" I protested.

"You'll do as you're told, and be quick about it," the first mate replied.

"It's all right, Miss Patience," Chips said quietly.

"You keep your nose out of this," ordered Bridgewater. He gave a violent sneeze and looked around wildly. "And where is that blasted cat?"

Binyon returned with Papa's bag and thrust it at me.

"Keep an eye on these two," said Bridgewater, his

eyes watering. "I don't trust them." He bared his teeth at me in one of his awful smiles. "And when you're done there, my dear, I fancy some of your biscuits for breakfast."

I was counting on this, and ducked my head to hide a smile as he headed aft. With Binyon breathing down my neck, though, I didn't know how I was going to fish what I needed out of Papa's bag. Opening the clasp, I peered inside, then reached in gingerly, careful to avoid the sharp razors and other metal instruments that lurked in its leathery depths.

Pulling out bandages and a stout needle and thread, I asked for fresh water. Binyon looked around, but there was no one else in sight to relay the order to.

"Just fetch it, will you, Binyon," I said crossly. "We aren't going anywhere."

I watched him as he crossed to the scuttlebutt and picked up a bucket and the dipper, then moved slightly so that my back was toward him.

"William Thomas, whatever possessed you!" I whispered angrily, reaching inside the bag again and patting the contents. Where was it? I flinched as something sharp stabbed my wrist. "I told Charlie to *fake* an accident."

Chips shook his head slightly. "They'd have twigged us for sure, Miss Patience," he whispered back. "That boy blushes like a rosebud."

He had a point. "Ha! Got it!" I said, as my hand closed around a small glass bottle.

"He's coming," whispered Chips, watching as I drew it out of the bag and slipped it into my pinafore pocket. He lifted an eyebrow questioningly.

"Laudanum," I whispered. He still looked puzzled. "You'll see."

Binyon came up behind me and handed over the bucket of water. I spared a glance at the ring of keys that hung from his belt. How was I going to free Chips? Without him, I didn't know if my plan would succeed. But Binyon was watching me like a hawk, and I couldn't see how to get the keys. I'd have to think of something else.

I washed the blood from the carpenter's forearm and, wishing fervently that I'd paid more attention to Mama's needlework instruction, stitched up the gash as carefully as I could, then bandaged it securely.

"Thank you, Miss Patience," said Chips.

"You're welcome."

Binyon poked me with his foot. "Into the galley with you now," he said in a surly voice, snatching back Papa's bag. "You heard the captain."

Glum was already at work stoking the woodstove, and when I was sure that Binyon and Bridgewater weren't looking, I caught his eye and pulled the laudanum bottle from my pocket. Glum took it from me curiously, uncorked it and surreptitiously sniffed the contents.

His eyes widened in surprise, and then his face split into a broad grin. "Well done, Miss Patience," he whispered, his voice brimming with admiration.

A cheerful Glum was an unusual sight, and quickly attracted Binyon's attention.

"What have you got to be so chipper about?" he asked suspiciously, coming over to investigate.

Glum's face instantly resumed its habitual undertaker's aspect.

"Nothing at all," he droned in his normal funereal tone.

"And what's that behind your back?"

I froze. We were discovered!

But Glum was cleverer than that.

"This, you mean?" he asked, holding up a jar of Martha's preserves. Looking beyond him, I spied the laudanum bottle sitting on the counter. He must have switched the two.

Bridgewater suddenly materialized at Binyon's elbow. "Plum jam?" he cried. "Have you been hiding this from me? I should have you flogged!"

Thrusting the jar into his coat pocket, he turned to me. "And shouldn't you be milking that wretched goat, if we're to have anything at all to eat this morning?"

I ducked my head, grabbed the waiting bucket and fled past him. Charlie and Mr. Macy were both on deck now; Charlie mutely bearing up under Binyon's jibes, and Mr. Macy gamely trying to keep up with the stream of orders that was being issued. I gave them both a quick smile.

Sprigg was gathering eggs, and seeing that Binyon's attention was elsewhere, I sidled up to him cautiously.

"Keep your eyes peeled today, Sprigg," I whispered. "Glum and I have a surprise up our sleeves."

He bent his head toward me and I quickly outlined our plan. When I finished he let out a delighted cackle.

"Should have known you wouldn't just sit there like a frog on a riverbank," he wheezed.

Binyon swaggered over and gave him a kick that sent him sprawling.

"Here now, there's no need for that!" cried Sprigg indignantly. "And look what you've done—two eggs broke, and them hens are laying few enough as it is!"

"Get back to work, the both of you," Binyon ordered.

Leaving Sprigg to cluck over his eggs, I turned my attention to Daisy. The goat was clearly pining for Thaddeus, as her milk supply had dwindled in recent days, and I was barely able to squeeze enough out of her for a decent batch of biscuits. I carried the bucket back to the galley and there, under Glum's watchful guard, surreptitiously substituted the entire contents of the bottle of laudanum for the usual dose of vinegar.

Behind me Bridgewater sneezed again and I jumped, dropping the empty bottle with a clatter.

"That cat is lurking about somewhere, I know it!" he cried. "Binyon!"

While the two of them were busy hunting Ishmael, I quickly bent down and picked up the bottle, then slipped it into my pinafore pocket. Glancing out the galley doorway I spotted my cat creeping forward. Unfortunately so did Bridgewater.

"Aha! I have you at last!" he said, and pounced.

But once again Ishmael proved too quick for him and darted by in a flash of gray fur. Bridgewater was struck with a fresh fit of sneezing, and while he was thus distracted Charlie Fishback scooped up my cat and tossed him to safety down the steerage hatch. Relieved, I waggled my fingers at him and smiled.

The biscuits were finished in short order, and my mouth watered when Glum removed them from the oven, puffed high and golden brown. He split one and gave me half, and we each took a bite.

"Ugh!" I said, and spat it out. We looked at each other, horrified. Glutton that he was, even Bridgewater couldn't help but notice the bitter aftertaste. What were we going to do?

"We'll just have to hope he likes plum jam," whispered Glum.

He set about preparing eggs and ham while I piled the biscuits onto a platter. Seeing Todd emerge to stand the next watch, I set a few aside as insurance.

Bridgewater was pacing the deck when Glum and I finally emerged bearing breakfast.

"It's about time!" he cried, plucking a biscuit from the platter. "Bear a hand, Sprigg, and help the girl take this down to the table. And fetch Binyon and Mr. Macy to join me."

He headed for the companionway.

"Greedy beggar," muttered Glum.

"How do you plan to warn Mr. Macy?" rasped Sprigg, as he took one of the breakfast trays.

"Leave that to me," I replied.

Below I lingered at the table while Sprigg went to fetch the others, rearranging the coffee pot and fussing with the napkins.

"Belay that hovering—don't you have pots to wash?" snapped Bridgewater, who, I was relieved to notice, was slathering Martha's plum preserves on the biscuit in his hand.

I lingered another minute until I heard the others start down the companionway, then ran up, brushing past Binyon and halting just in front of the third mate. Hesitating just long enough to allow Binyon to reach the bottom, I pretended to lurch as the *Morning Star* rolled, and flung myself toward Mr. Macy.

"Steady as she goes, Miss Patience!" he said.

"Oh excuse me, Mr. Macy," I replied loudly, crumpling in a heap at his feet.

"Are you all right?" he asked, bending down to help me up.

I grabbed the arm of his jacket and pulled him closer. "Don't eat the biscuits," I said in an urgent whisper.

He looked at me, puzzled. "But—"

I jerked my head toward the table, where Bridgewater, cheeks bulging with biscuit, was chewing vigorously.

"Ah, yes," said Mr. Macy. "I see." He smiled at me. "And you have a lovely morning as well, Miss Patience."

Back on deck the lingering scent of ham drew Todd to the galley like a cat to a dead fish.

"'E never orders ham the mornings I joins 'im," he grumbled.

"I can't do anything about the ham," I said crossly, and with feigned reluctance handed him the biscuits I had reserved. "I was saving these for later, but if you'll promise to be nicer to Charlie I'll let you have them instead."

He laughed nastily and snatched the plate from me. "Saving them for your sweetheart, were you?" he said. "I'll make no promises of the sort."

And turning, he bit into one and hollered, "You there! Firetop! As a special favor to the cook's helper here, I'll let you muck out the hogpen this morning!"

Glum and I watched with apprehension as he chewed loudly for a moment, then screwed up his face in disgust.

"Pah!" he said, spitting it out. "This is 'orrible!"

Picking up another one, he nibbled on it tentatively, then stepped to the siderail and flung the entire contents of the plate into the water below.

"Even the hogs wouldn't eat them biscuits," he declared angrily.

Glum was silent, and as I struggled to wipe the guilty expression off my face, my hand unconsciously slipped into my pinafore pocket and closed around the now-empty bottle of laudanum.

Todd looked at us speculatively. "Are you two up to something?" he asked.

I shook my head vigorously, but he advanced toward us, eyes narrowing with suspicion. "I believe you are," he said.

Glum gave me a shove that nearly sent me sprawling. "What are you waiting for, girl?" he bellowed. "You've got dishes to wash!"

Startled by his rudeness, I glared at him, but he tossed me a reassuring wink as he stepped between me and Todd. I moved to the far corner of the galley.

"Out of the way, cook," said Todd in a steely voice. His pistol had appeared in his hand, and he shouldered Glum aside. "And you come here, missy."

Knees shaking, I moved reluctantly toward him. Grabbing me by the shoulder, he pulled me out of the galley and shook me until my teeth rattled.

"You're a sly baggage, you are. I'll wager you've been up to something."

"I don't know what you're talking about!"

"Leave her be, Todd," growled Glum. "If there's any fault with the biscuits, it's that blasted goat. Her milk's been off these past few days."

Todd didn't take his eyes off of me, but he lowered the pistol. "The goat, is it?" he said. He chewed his lip speculatively. "We'll see about that. Down below with you, missy. Best let the cap'n decide."

I looked at Glum frantically as Todd gripped my arm and dragged me toward the companionway. He started after me, but Todd waved the pistol at him menacingly. "Stay where you are, cook. This doesn't concern you."

Binyon and Mr. Macy looked up in surprise as we clattered down the stairs into the main cabin. Todd shoved me forward. "This minx is up to summat," he announced.

"Is that so?" drawled Bridgewater, yawning. He shoved another biscuit into his mouth. "And what might that be?"

Todd hesitated, watching in fascination as Bridgewater chewed and swallowed. "It's, it's—well, it's them biscuits, sir."

"The biscuits?" Bridgewater blinked at him sleepily. "Fine biscuits, as always. Make us another batch while you're at it, Miss Patience." His head bobbed onto his chest. "Meanwhile, I do believe I'll take a little nap."

And with another yawn he slowly keeled forward onto the table, landing with his face planted squarely in the dish of Martha's plum preserves. Nobody said a word for a long moment.

"I tell you, Binyon, she's done summat to the biscuits," insisted Todd, as Bridgewater let out a loud snore.

Mr. Macy snickered, and Binyon looked at him angrily. "You haven't et any biscuits this morning, I notice," he said accusingly. "Maybe Todd is right."

Binyon thrust out a grubby finger and prodded Bridgewater, who merely snuffled in the jam. With a glance in my direction, he took the last biscuit from the plate. Bridgewater snored again, and I tried my best to look guileless as Binyon peered at the biscuit suspiciously, then sniffed it and gave it a lick.

"Go on then, take a bite," urged Todd.

Cautiously Binyon did so, chewed for a moment, and then spat it onto the floor with an oath. Pushing back from the table, he stood up slowly, menacingly, and I quailed as his bulk seemed to block the sun from the skylight above. He crooked a finger at me.

"Come here," he ordered. Todd shoved me forward again.

"I say, gentlemen, don't you think you're making a mountain out of a molehill?" asked Mr. Macy, his Adam's apple bobbing nervously.

"Shut up," said Binyon tersely. He squeezed my shoulder in an iron fist. "What did you do to them biscuits?"

My heart was beating wildly. I didn't know what to say or what to do! The best I could hope for now was that they'd believe Glum's story about the goat and lock me back in my cabin again. I didn't want to think about what they'd do to me if they discovered the truth.

Without warning, Binyon picked me up, slung me over his shoulder and started for the companionway. "Perhaps a little dip will get you to talk," he said.

He was going to throw me overboard!

"No!" I yelled. "Put me down!"

I began to struggle frantically, and as I did so the laudanum bottle slipped from my pocket and fell to the floor. Todd pounced on it with a screech of triumph.

"'Ere, didn't I tell you," he cried.

Binyon dropped me with a thud and grabbed the bottle from his companion's hand. He sniffed the contents.

"Laudanum," he said in disgust.

As he turned again toward me, I shrank back in fear. His face wore a truly malevolent expression. "Right then," he said. "I've had about enough of you."

He dove for me, but I was too quick for him. Ducking between his legs, I scrambled to my feet and pounded up the companionway. He was right on my heels, his hands clutching at my skirt. Gasping, I emerged into the sunlight, but he grabbed my ankle and I sprawled forward.

He loomed over me, grinning broadly, and I gave a cry of fright. Before he could grab me, however, a shadow fell across the deck as Glum emerged from behind the companionway, frypan in hand. He raised it in the air and thwacked Binyon on the back of the head with it.

The tall sailor toppled forward, landing beside me with a mighty crash. He lay there, motionless and groaning. The keys! I thought. I scrambled over to him and plucked the keyring from off his belt, then rolled out of the way again just as Todd appeared, blinking in the bright sun. When he saw his companion lying on the deck, he lifted his pistol.

"Move away from him, the both of you," he ordered. "And you put that down now, cook."

Reluctantly Glum set down his frypan. I rose to my feet and we retreated toward the galley. Todd stepped forward and prodded Binyon with his toe. "You all right, then?"

Binyon groaned again and my heart sank as I saw that he had managed to push himself up on all fours.

Just then Mr. Macy launched himself from the companionway with a battle cry, landing on Todd's back. As they collided the pistol fired wildly, then fell to the deck with a clatter and skittered just beyond reach of either of them. I wasted no time in racing back toward the mainmast where Chips still sat in irons.

"Here, Miss Patience!" he cried when he saw me. "Toss them to me!"

I threw him the keys and he caught them. Behind me, Binyon had managed to lurch to his feet. Todd and Mr. Macy were still wrestling frantically for the weapon. Binyon stood there a moment, swaying, looking first at them and then at me. Glum grabbed me by the back of my pinafore and shoved me behind him into the galley.

"Keep your head down," he warned.

Binyon turned his attention to the struggling pair, but as he started for them the door of the deck house opened and a wiry ankle shot out. Binyon tripped over it and fell again, landing on Mr. Macy. With a cackle of glee, Sprigg sprang out of hiding, pigtail flying wildly and spectacles askew. Behind him was Charlie Fishback. While Sprigg scuttled off after the pistol, Chips appeared and pulled Binyon off of Mr. Macy. Charlie sat on Todd.

Another shot rang out.

"Don't either of you slimy bilge rats move an inch," screeched Sprigg with a piratical leer. Binyon and Todd froze. "Where's that reptile Bridgewater?"

A thunderous snore wafted up the companionway.

"I believe he's safe for the moment," wheezed Mr. Macy, standing up gingerly and dusting himself off. "Let's tie these two up and take them below."

"Wait!" I said, stepping out of the galley. "I have a better idea."

Everyone looked at me. Grabbing a length of rope and passing it to Chips, I continued, "Don't you think these two ought to be taught a lesson? A *swimming* lesson?"

Understanding dawned and Chips smiled broadly. "Right you are, Miss Patience."

Quicker than Jack Flash, he wrapped the line

around Binyon and Todd and secured the end of it to the taffrail.

"Just a moment, Chips," I said, and stepping up to Binyon, whipped my silver dollar from his neck. "I'll take that, Bunion."

He glowered at me, but his hands were tied fast and the line was secure in Chips's keeping. With Charlie Fishback's help, Chips bundled him and his companion over the stern of the *Morning Star*. They hit the water with a mighty splash and bobbed up again like two bags of soiled laundry, spluttering and protesting.

"But I can't swim!" wailed Todd.

"Shut up, you fool!" said Binyon, clinging desperately to the rope.

"It's all in jest," I called down to them.

"We don't mean you any harm, lads," added Chips helpfully, and the two of us collapsed against each other, laughing heartily, much to the mystification of the others.

"It's a private joke," I explained, still giggling.

Our shipmates joined us at the taffrail, and we all watched for a bit in great satisfaction as the *Morning Star* dragged the gurgling pair in her wake.

"That'll take the wind out of their sails," said Sprigg, peering at them over his spectacles.

"And they'll be nice and clean," added Glum.

I felt a rush of affection for my companions. Papa was right, after all. A ship's crew *was* like a family, and together we had done what we never could have managed alone.

"Huzzah for the *Morning Star!*" I cried with feeling, and the others took up the cheer.

"And huzzah for Miss Patience!" said Chips, as Charlie Fishback clapped me on the back.

"And don't forget the biscuits!" added Mr. Macy.

"Huzzah for the biscuits!" we all cried, and went below to deal with Bridgewater.

Eighteen

Our ship seems conscious of the hour
That proves her strength and sailing power.
She swiftly plows the parting tide,
Her captain's and her seamen's pride.

—*Now We Steer Our Course for Home*

June 20, 1836

With Bilgewater, Bunion, and Toad safely in irons and stowed in the lower hold like so many sacks of grain, the Morning Star *is ours again.*

Now it only remains to be seen if I can guide us back to where Papa, Thaddeus, and the others await our return. I have taken over our quarters again, and am even now consulting Papa's charts.

We are sadly shorthanded, for Bilgewater was wont to press Bunion and Toad into service these past days when the weather demanded it, but Glum and Chips are willing to take a trick at the wheel, and Sprigg swears that although age has diminished his sight, it overlooked his arms and legs, and says he's as ready as any man aboard to nip aloft and reef sail.

*Pray God give us clear skies and a fair wind,
so we do not lose heart.*

—*P.*

For a week we sailed back in the direction from which we had come. Fortune indeed smiled upon us, and the days unfurled like a strand of flawless pearls, unmarred by squalls or fog.

Unfortunately there was no one aboard to help me with the navigation. I had hoped to rely on Mr. Macy, who as senior officer aboard found himself unexpectedly thrust into command, but though he tried diligently, Cousin Jeremiah was right: My own modest skills were well in advance of his, and he only got in a muddle.

Each day at noon I took an observation with my sextant, nervously checking and rechecking my numbers, then disappeared below to sit hunched over Papa's desk with his *Practical Navigator,* charts, *Nautical Almanac,* and my pencil. I was not yet skilled enough to be able to fix longitude, but latitude was not beyond my grasp. At least I hoped it was not.

Knowing that Bridgewater had taken the *Morning Star* southeast again from where he left Papa, making for the port of Talcahuano, my plan was to sail directly north until we reached the latitude of Papa's island, then simply veer west again and sail along that parallel until we found it. It was dead reckoning of the most elementary sort, and liable to error, but it was the only way that I could fathom in which to find them.

Sleep eluded me; I tossed and turned in my bunk, worried that the task was beyond me, and fearful that my original sighting had been wrong. Even a degree or two could mean the difference between success and failure, and if I failed, we could crisscross the seas for weeks, searching in vain for the tiny island where Papa and Thaddeus and the others were marooned.

Not even the balmy tropical nights could cheer me, beautiful though they were, with skies as black as wet whaleskin and stars that hung low and close, like apples ripe for the picking. I paced the deck for hours in the moonlight, never failing to search for the North Star and thinking now of Papa and Tad as well as Mama.

Mama was often in my thoughts, and in my fitful slumber I sometimes thought I could hear her calling my name.

"Patience," she would whisper. "Patience."

I would sit up in my bunk. "Mama!" I would call back, straining to hear her reply in the darkness.

But it was only the wind in the rigging.

The crew did their best to keep my spirits up. Mr. Macy's orders, which daily grew in confidence and a noticeable absence of squeaks, were cheerfully obeyed; Glum ensured that our meals were hot and regular (with the exception of those carried below to Bridgewater and the others—"There can't be too many weevils in their duff," as Chips put it); and even Sprigg was unusually solicitous, anticipating my every need.

"May I bring you a cup of tea, Miss Patience?" he would say, or "Mind you get some rest, Miss Patience," fussing over me like a mother hen until I was driven nearly to distraction.

Day after day we sailed, until over a week had passed. We had only been five days under Bridgewater's command, and despite the intentionally circuitous route I had planned for us, I began to fear that my plan had failed. On the morning of the eighth day, I paced the deck and fidgeted, leaping near out of my skin when Charlie Fishback called out from the masthead, by force of habit more than anything else, "There she blows!"

"Whales we have no need of," I cried impatiently. "It's land you're looking for!"

He grinned and tipped his cap to me.

At noon I took another observation and raced below to Papa's desk. Holding my breath, I made the necessary corrections with the help of the chronometer and the *Practical Navigator,* then applied the declination of the sun from the *Nautical Almanac* to calculate our latitude yet again. Only when I saw that we were still at 2°40' S did I let out a sigh of relief. We were continuing to sail along the same parallel as Papa's island.

But why hadn't it been sighted yet—surely we *must* be nearing it by now! Could we have sailed past it in the night? Or what if my initial sextant reading had been all wrong and we were on a false course altogether? I gnawed at my thumbnail in an agony of indecision.

Brushing away the tray of food Glum had prepared for me, I went back up on deck, weighing the risks of having Mr. Macy give orders to double back. Instead, ignoring the screech that burst forth from Sprigg, I tucked my skirt and petticoat and pinafore up into my pantaloons and climbed into the rigging.

Quicker than Jack Flash, the steward was right behind me. "Hoyden!" he called. "Come down from there this instant!"

I ignored him and continued upward. The island simply *had* to be there, and I was determined to find it. Breathless from his insistent squawking, Sprigg soon fell behind. When I arrived at the masthead Charlie reached down and pulled me up onto the platform.

"Good on you, Miss Patience!" he said, shaking my hand heartily.

"Still nothing, Charlie?" I replied, a bit breathless myself after the vigorous climb.

He shook his head. "But don't lose hope."

He passed me the spyglass, and I scanned the horizon. It stretched away to every point on the compass, as flat and blue as Mama's best tablecloth.

Sprigg's gray head poked up through the rigging. "Move aside there," he said waspishly.

It was a tight squeeze, but we managed to make room for him.

"The things a sailor finds himself called upon to do aboard this old tub," he muttered in disgust.

Charlie suppressed a smile and turned away. The three of us stood there, gazing unblinkingly in different directions.

"Not that I could see a thing anyway," complained Sprigg after a bit, blinking feebly through his spectacles.

I handed him Papa's spyglass. "Here," I said. "Try this."

Grumbling still, he took it from me, then fell silent. The minutes ticked by. It seemed as if an eternity passed. Below, I could hear Mr. Macy calling to Chips, who was at the helm, and a clatter of pots from the galley where Glum was cleaning up from breakfast.

And then, "Don't suppose that's it," said Sprigg in an offhand manner.

"Where?" I said, whipping around.

He pointed in front of him. "Off the larboard bow."

I snatched the spyglass away from him, holding my breath as I squinted through the eyepiece. Nothing but sky and sea at first, and then a faint, ever so faint, smudge swam into my vision, blurring as tears filled my eyes. It had to be land!

"Oh, Sprigg, bless you, I think you've found it!" I said, and throwing my arms around him, gave him a smacking kiss on his wrinkled cheek.

"That's quite enough of that," he said with his usual peevishness, but I could tell he was pleased.

Cupping my hands around my mouth, I called down to Mr. Macy, "Land! Land ho! Sprigg found it!"

A cheer arose from below as the men heard the news.

"Where away?" hollered Mr. Macy.

"Three points off the larboard bow!" Charlie called back in return, and the third mate gave us a wave to show that he'd heard.

"We'd best get down now, Miss Patience," said Sprigg. "Mr. Macy'll be crowding on sail quicker than—"

"Jack Flash?" I finished with a smile.

He peered at me over his spectacles.

"Congratulations, Miss Patience," said Charlie, as

Sprigg ducked through the masthoops and, mumbling under his breath about the impertinence of girls who weren't half as clever as they imagined, began his descent. "I knew you could do it."

"Enough nabbering up there. Come along now, the both of you!" Sprigg grabbed my ankle as I lowered myself down, and placed my foot firmly in the rigging. "Mind where you put your feet, or we'll be scraping you off the deck with Glum's dustpan."

Once we were safely below, Mr. Macy indeed gave the order to hoist more sail. "I want every scrap of canvas aboard this ship aloft to catch the breeze!" he bellowed, his voice suddenly surprisingly deep and robust. "Topgallants and royals, staysails and spanker—clap onto those lines, men, and haul for all you're worth!"

Soon, her wings spread to their fullest, the *Morning Star* surged forward with renewed energy. Gradually, the smudge on the horizon grew larger.

"Keep her steady on her course, Chips!" called Mr. Macy.

"Aye, sir!" the carpenter replied.

Impatiently I raced forward and planted myself at the bow, grasping the forestay firmly as Papa had shown me. Jubilant, I faced toward the island on the horizon, my hair streaming behind me in the wind. We had found it!

Worry still gnawed at me, however. What if Papa

and Thaddeus and the others weren't there? What if they had been picked up by another ship, or kidnapped by savages? Or what if there was indeed no water on the island and they had perished?

As we drew closer, the crew began to join me one by one—first Glum, then Sprigg, one on either side of me like a pair of dour bookends, then Mr. Macy and Charlie—even Domingo and Antonio. All but Chips, who stood faithfully at the wheel, holding us to our course. No one spoke a word.

Finally we were close enough to make out the shape of the rocky shore. I took Papa's spyglass from my pocket and, sending a silent prayer heavenward, raised it to my eye with a shaking hand.

Adjusting the focus, I scanned the island, moving the lens slowly, agonizingly slowly along the beach so as not to overlook anything.

"They *must* be there," I whispered over the lump in my throat. But there was nothing.

I scanned the island again, and my spirits plummeted. They weren't there—there was nothing but rocks and sand. I had failed! I started to lower the spyglass, and then—

"Wait!" I breathed, raising it to my eye again and adjusting the focus. "I think I see something!"

"Well, don't leave us all hanging by our thumbs," cried Sprigg. "What is it? Is it them?"

"I see Papa and Tad!" I sobbed, tears of relief and exhaustion and gratitude running down my face. Glum reached out and gathered me in his skinny arms. "I see Papa and Tad!"

Epilogue

June 28, 1836

Papa has entered me into his logbook.

"On this, the twenty-eighth day of June, in the year of our Lord 1836," he wrote in a careful hand, "I, Captain Isaiah Goodspeed, along with my son Thaddeus and fourteen loyal members of the crew of the bark Morning Star, *were rescued from certain death by the grace of God and my daughter, Patience, being thirteen years of age and as stout of heart and quick of mind as any man that ever sailed forth from the island of Nantucket."*

Then he signed his name below with a flourish.

"Thunder and lightning, Patience! You're a Goodspeed through and through," he proclaimed, and embraced me warmly.

Life aboard our small ship has resumed its

happy routine, all of us gladly taking up the mantle of our former duties. Mr. Chase is acting as first mate now, and Mr. Macy has been promoted to second. We are without a third mate at present, though Papa says he's keeping an eye on Charlie Fishback.

The Morning Star's *course is set for Lahaina, a port on the island of Maui, where we will have a proper rest and where Papa will deliver Bilgewater and his fellow mutineers to the consul. Papa assures me they will be dealt with most severely.*

They continue below in the lower hold, a sullen trio and an unpleasantly damp one as well, for the waters of the bilge are notoriously slimy. When they learned they would not be moved to more comfortable quarters, Bunion and Toad protested most loudly, until Chips went down and tossed a bucket of cold seawater onto them and told them to stop their caterwauling, and that there was plenty more where that came from. Not a peep have we heard from them since, except for the occasional sneeze from Bilgewater. Ishmael merely flicks his tail and blinks at me when I ask him if he's intentionally gallying our prisoner, but I think that the answer is yes.

Thaddeus continues to keep Sprigg hopping,

but since his days marooned ashore he has grown much attached to Papa and spends most of his hours trailing in his wake. That is as it should be.

As for me, Papa has bestowed yet another honor upon me.

I am now assistant navigator, and though I still find myself in the galley making pies and biscuits with Glum, helping Papa chart our course is my primary duty, one for which Papa promises I will be amply rewarded when we reach our destination.

Even more dear to me, however, is the fact that although Papa is still prickly and proud and given to flashes of temper (as am I on occasion as well, I must confess), we are truly a family once again. And our small family is firmly fixed within the larger family of the Morning Star as well, encircled by bonds forged from shared tragedy and triumph.

There are none of the lingering shadows of grief that clung to us when we left home those many months ago either, and Papa mentions Mama freely now. "She would be so proud of you," he tells me again and again—and while she is still often in my thoughts, it is with joy and not sadness that I recall her gentle spirit, some of which I hope she has bequeathed to me.

Too, I have come to see that Papa was right.

My place is aboard the Morning Star, *and he
and Thaddeus and I were meant to be together—
Goodspeeds through and through!*

*Papa promises that it will ever be this way,
and that the three of us will sail together for as
long as there are whales in the sea.*

—P.

Author's Note

This story began entirely by fluke, if you'll pardon the pun. Several years ago, my great-uncle Billy (William H. H. Fishback of Harwich, Massachusetts) sent me a copy of a family document that would launch me on a voyage of discovery whose outcome I could not even imagine at the time.

It was a receipt for whaling gear for my great-great-grandfather, Charles Fishback (whose name I couldn't resist filching for one of the characters in this book), sent from a New Bedford outfitter to Charles's father, John, back in Batavia, Ohio. The total was $84.93—a sizeable sum in those days. Imagine how furious John Fishback must have been to discover that not only had his fifteen-year-old son run away from home, but that he'd also been stuck with the bill for the escapade! (To his credit, John paid in full.)

Charles shipped out on the bark *Midas* of New Bedford on November 1, 1865, just a few months after the end of the Civil War. He wouldn't see the shores of his homeland again until March 24, 1869, some three and a half years later. It was a successful voyage commercially, but I wondered what it was like personally for young Charles. Surely he must have been homesick, seasick, overworked, underfed—and very likely scared out of his wits at times. Like many nineteenth-century farm boys, he was probably lured to sea by advertisements that exaggerated the opportunities whaling afforded for advancement and adventure, but remained silent about the danger and privation sailors would face.

While reading more about this eventful chapter in American history, I quickly stumbled upon a fascinating fact. Because a typical whaling cruise lasted anywhere from two to five years, ships' captains would frequently take their wives—and sometimes their whole families—along with them. The idea for *The Voyage of Patience Goodspeed* was sparked right then and there.

Although Patience's adventures are the stuff of fiction, many details were inspired by real-life historical events (such as the sinking of the whaleship *Essex* in 1820 by a whale) and people. Maria Mitchell, Patience's math tutor, was America's first woman astronomer and one of Nantucket's most famous citizens. She really did run a school on the island, and eventually became a professor of astronomy at Vassar College. In 1836 she was hired as librarian for the Nantucket Atheneum (though for the purpose of my story, I allowed her to start a few months earlier, in the fall of 1835). Many of the places I visited for research pop up in Patience's tale as well—the poem Mr. Macy recites at Long Tom's funeral service, for instance, comes from an epitaph engraved on a marble tablet on the wall of the Seaman's Bethel in New Bedford.

As for the whales themselves, there's no doubt in my mind that these magnificent creatures are best "hunted" with a camera from the deck of a sightseeing boat. Over the years, the whaling industry drove many species to the brink of extinction. Today, however, thanks to international conservation efforts, their populations have recovered significantly, but vigilant protection is still needed to ensure their survival.

And what of my great-great-grandfather? He became a skilled seaman, shipping out on several more whaling cruises and rising to the position of boatsteerer to the third mate. Eventually he earned his master's papers for ocean sail and steam, piloting boats along the eastern seaboard before settling down to skipper a Nantucket ferry. Charles is buried alongside his wife, Sarah, in Nantucket's Prospect Hill cemetery.

Patience's Biscuits

*"There were smiles all around today when I appeared
with a platter piled high with hot biscuits."*

2 cups flour

3 teaspoons baking powder

1 teaspoon salt

1/3 cup lard (or vegetable shortening)

3/4 cup buttermilk (if buttermilk is unavailable,

add 1 tablespoon vinegar to regular milk to

make it sour)

Preheat the oven to 450°F. Mix the dry ingredients together. Cut in the lard or shortening with a
pastry blender or 2 knives until the mixture resem-
bles fine crumbs. Stir in the buttermilk just until
blended. Turn the dough onto a lightly floured surface and knead gently until the dough forms a
smooth ball. Roll out a 1/2 inch thick and cut into
circles with a biscuit or cookie cutter.

Place biscuits close together, edges touching, on
a cookie sheet. Bake at 450°F for 10 to 12 minutes
or until the tops of the biscuits are golden brown.
Serve piping hot, preferably with lots of butter and
honey or homemade jam.

Glum's Favorite Gingersnaps

"Cheered by the prospect of gingersnaps, his favorite treat, Glum grew unusually expansive."

3/4 cup vegetable shortening

1 1/3 cups sugar

1 egg

1/4 cup molasses

2 teaspoons baking soda

2 cups flour

1/4 teaspoon salt

1 teaspoon cinnamon

1 teaspoon cloves

1 teaspoon ginger

Extra sugar in which to roll cookies

Preheat the oven to 350°F. Cream the shortening and sugar together. Add the remaining ingredients and blend together. Chill the dough for at least 1 hour. Form small balls with it and roll them in sugar, then place them on a cookie sheet about 2 to 3 inches apart. Bake at 350°F for 10 to 12 minutes.

Glossary

aft, or after: at or toward the stern of a ship

bark: a ship with three masts, whose sails are square-rigged (perpendicular to the deck) on the fore- and mainmasts and fore-and-aft rigged (parallel to the deck) on the mizzenmast

bilge: the lowest part of the ship's interior

blanket piece: a long strip of blubber cut or ripped from the whale

boatsteerer: another name for harpooneer, so called because after striking the whale with his harpoon, he trades places with the mate and steers the whaleboat

cat-o'-nine-tails: a knotted rope with which seamen could be flogged for punishment

chronometer: a highly accurate clock set to Greenwich mean time

companionway: a ship's staircase that leads from one deck to another

cooper: the crew member responsible for making wooden casks or barrels for storing whale oil and supplies

cutting in: the process of removing blubber from a whale

fo'c'sle: abbreviation for "forecastle," the front part of a ship belowdecks where the crew's quarters are located

fore, or forward: the front part of ship, toward the bow

foremast: the mast nearest the bow, or front, of a ship

gaff: a large hook on a pole

galley: a ship's kitchen

gam: a social visit between crews of whaling ships

green hand or greenie: an inexperienced seaman

gurry: a smelly mixture of seawater, rancid whale oil, and whale innards

halyard: a rope used to hoist or lower a sail

larboard: the port or left-hand side of a ship

lighter: a small barge used to ferry cargo and passengers from ship to shore

logbook: the official record of a ship's voyage

mainmast: a ship's tallest mast; the center mast in a three-masted ship

masthoop: an iron circle attached to the masthead to protect the lookout from falling

mizzenmast: the mast nearest the stern in a three-masted ship

reef: to take in or shorten a sail

Sandwich Islands: nineteenth-century name for the Hawaiian Islands

scuttlebutt: a cask placed in a central part of a ship for drinking water

sextant: a navigational instrument for measuring the angular distance of the sun, moon, or stars from the horizon

spoke: past tense of speak, the term used to describe the hailing of another ship

starboard: the right-hand side of a ship

stern: the rear part of a ship

taffrail: the rail around the stern of a ship

try-pot: large cauldron or pot in which blubber is boiled

tryworks: a furnacelike stove built out of brick that holds the try-pots

waist: the part of the upper deck between the fore- and mainmasts

whaleboat: a long, open rowboat, pointed at both ends like a canoe and launched from a ship to chase whales

Acknowledgments

There are many people to whom I owe a debt of gratitude in writing this novel. First and foremost is my husband, Steve Frederick, whose love, support, and encouragement have always provided me safe harbor. Lisa Carper, my sister, was a cheerful companion and chauffeur on several research expeditions around maritime New England. My father, Stefan Vogel, has ever been my musical inspiration, and I appreciate his assistance in finding sources for some of the sea shanties that introduce each chapter. My great-uncle William H. Fishback's careful stewardship of family history is the rock on which this story was built (and for the record, I consider "Bill Fish" and his cousin "Dolly B," aka Dorothy Boyer Gornick, two of New Bedford and Nantucket's finest). Elizabeth Devereaux gallantly served as first reader and bolstered my confidence at a critical early stage, while Kevin Lewis and Alyssa Eisner—brilliant navigators both—helped steer the project to completion. Susan Blackaby, my writing group of one, is always there for tea-and-sympathy dates, and I may as well try to number the stars as attempt to recount friend and fairy godsister Cyndi Howard's innumerable kindnesses.

Laura Pereira, Library Assistant at the Old Dartmouth Historical Society in New Bedford, Massachusetts, generously allowed an amateur historian with nothing more to recommend her than clean hands and a pure heart free access to invaluable whaling journals and other material. Michael Dyer, Curator of Maritime History at Kendall Whaling Museum in Sharon, Massachusetts, set me straight on ship's idlers and the waters where various species of whales may be found. Thanks, too, to Donald Treworgy, Planetarium Director at Mystic Seaport, for help with celestial navigation terminology; to his colleague Rachel Thomas, research associate extraordinaire, for vetting the manuscript; and to Jim Blackaby and all the other staff members at Mystic. Invaluable, too, was the help I received from those at the New Bedford Whaling Museum, the Nantucket Whaling Museum, and the Nantucket Atheneum. Any factual errors that remain are entirely of my own doing.

Finally, I am most appreciative of a 1999 grant from Literary Arts, Inc., of Portland, Oregon, that allowed me to move Patience and her shipmates from a box full of note cards onto the pages of this book.